The Keeala Series

The Last Resort

Kumari Gorman

By the same author

The Keeala Resort Series

Book 2 - Village Secrets

Book 3 - The Road Home

Book 4 - Crystal Clear

The Keeala Resort Series

The Last Resort

© Kumari Gorman 2014

National Library of Australia Cataloguing-in-Publication entry (pbk)

Author:	Gorman, Kumari, author.
Title:	The Last Resort/ Kumari Gorman.
ISBN:	9780992388003 (paperback)
Series:	Gorman, Kumari. Keeala Resort Series
Subjects:	Resorts—Queensland--Fiction

Dewey Number: A823.4

Published with the assistance by www.inhousepublishing.com.au

The Keeala Series

The Last Resort

Acknowledgements.

I would like to thank Ocean Reeve for his wonderful words of wisdom and his freely given support. He arrived at a time when I was about to give up. He guided me back on to the right track and I am very grateful that he inspired me to keep going. Thank you Ocean.

To my husband, John. Thank you so much. Thank you for your time, patience, advice and support.

Well, for some of your time and patience.

Well, perhaps tolerance is a better word.

Maybe I mean a bit of your time and occasional patience.

Definitely some tolerance and some occasional advice.

Whatever. You know what I mean.

Kumari Gorman

October 2014.

Chapter One

L aurie Lyall's day did not begin quite the way he expected.

As sunrise shafted out of the horizon, it fanfared a hail of bullets and shotgun pellets that shattered the early morning torpor. Splintery holes appeared from left to right across the front of his timber house. Glass exploded in the sliding doors on the veranda and shredded the sheer curtains. A second later, the main bedroom windows burst into a lacerating rain of shards. The vertical blinds, closed for the morning sun behind the glass, swung in tangled, peppered disarray.

An old Ford V8 roared away and left a cloud of acrid smoke as it laid snaking strips of burnt rubber down the asphalt. Its rear end spun out, then recovered, as it drifted left around a corner and joined the motorway on-ramp at the end of the street. Within seconds it was gone, the throbbing boom of its eight cylinders swallowed into the din of the early morning motorway traffic.

Dogs barked and howled at the shattering intrusion. A woman's scream merged with the cries of children. Other voices joined and swelled the commotion.

Laurie Lyall stumbled out of bed, but recovered his balance and hung onto the bedroom door for support.

"Jesus, Marian, are you OK?" He looked at his wife.

"Yeah, yeah, I'm OK. What the hell's going on?" she shouted, as she sat up. She saw the weak morning sun through holes punched in the walls and vertical blinds. A split second later, her motherly instinct clicked her brain into gear and she screamed, "My God, the kids!"

Laurie lurched toward the bedrooms at the back of the house. He shook the sleepiness from his head as he went. Two wide-eyed faces stared at him as he opened the door to the second bedroom.

"Just stay here, boys. Mum's coming. Stay here!" He moved to the third bedroom and picked up his daughter. "It's okay, love, it's okay. I want you to come and stay with Mum." As he came out of the bedroom with her in his arms, he saw Marian at the door of the second bedroom. He gave his daughter to her. "Stay in there with the kids, Marian. Stay there!"

Wide-awake now, adrenaline streamed through his body and heightened his senses. He turned around and ran toward the kitchen. His mobile phone was in a charger on the wall. He snatched it from its cradle as he went past and took three steps to the rear of the kitchen. Breathing hard, he unlocked the back door, but before he opened it, he peered through one of the two glass panels in the upper half. A quick look around the backyard was enough to satisfy his caution sufficiently for him to step slowly onto the back landing. Still wary, he paused, looked down into the yard, saw it was clear, and then took the back stairs, two at a time. At the bottom, he stepped off a concrete pad onto a coarse gravel path.

He looked down. Blood was running down his lower leg, yet the adrenaline had so fuelled his system that he felt no pain, not from his bare feet on the sharp edged gravel, or from the wound on his calf.

Laurie shook his head and continued on the gravel path to the side of the house. His heart was pounding as he stopped and looked up the narrow passageway between the house and the side fence. It too, was clear. Cautiously, he moved along the paved path toward the tall gate that gave access to the front yard. He reached the barrier, quietly disengaged the catch, and nudged the gate slightly ajar. He could see no one. After a few seconds, he pushed the gate slowly through its arc and opened up his field of view. Satisfied the area was clear, he stepped into the front yard. Glass fragments in the lawn sparkled as they caught the glow from the emerging sunlight.

He looked up and gasped as he saw the damage to his home. The door upstairs had nothing but jagged glass edges to adorn the distorted aluminium frame. Shreds of curtain gave a ragged backdrop. Bullet holes spread in an erratic line across the front of the house and shotgun pellets had concentrated holes around the main bedroom window on the top floor. For some seconds Laurie did not move, then, with a shake of his head, looked down at his phone and dialled 000.

A crowd gathered outside in the street. Fingers pointed, heads shook, questions hung in the air. There were no answers, just shrugs.

The police arrived at the house quickly; three cars, sirens wailing, lights flashing. Within a couple of minutes, police herded the onlookers behind crime scene tapes and barriers on the street. The front upstairs section of the house was overwhelmed with uniforms and noise. In the relative calm at the rear, a conversation was taking place.

"So, do you have any idea why anyone would want to do this?" was one of the first questions asked by the sergeant. He sat at the kitchen table with Laurie and his family. They could not use the chairs in the lounge room; shattered glass littered the room.

Marian cried. The three children sat nudging each other and giggling.

"No, I've no idea." Laurie looked away from the police officer and put his arm around his wife. He tried to reassure her. "It's over now, love, we're all okay." A quiver in his voice betrayed his confident tone.

Marian dabbed tears from her eyes with a crumpled tissue. "What about the protest last Saturday?" Marian sobbed.

Her husband looked down at her, shook his head slowly, and replied, without conviction, "Surely not."

"And what protest would that be, sir?" asked the sergeant. His tone left no doubt that he would not accept an evasive reply.

"Ah, well, ah, last week I headed a protest at the offices of the Sleighmen Group – in the city. We were protesting against the company's proposal to expand their Over 50's resort. They have plans to extend their Keeala Resort into the adjacent rural land." Laurie bit his lower lip and he could sense his face reddening as he looked away from the officer's piercing stare.

"Mmm, yeah, I know the place. So, you were objecting to the extension of the Over 50's Resort. I see." He scribbled a few words in his notebook. "And, when you say, *we were protesting*, who does the *we* refer to?"

Before Laurie could respond, Marian interrupted. "I knew that was just going to cause more trouble for us." She stood, blew her nose and then, with clenched fists held stiffly by her sides, she threw her head back and motioned to the kids to follow her from the room. "I've heard enough, Laurie. You're a born troublemaker and never listen to me, even if it means us all being killed, like just almost happened. You and your bloody eco warriors, you can all go to hell, the whole bloody lot of you." The door slammed behind her.

Embarrassed, Laurie lifted his eyes to the sergeant and sighed.

"The, *we*, sir?" the police officer asked again.

"It's a group of concerned citizens. We operate under the banner of CARP – Campaign Against the Rape of the Planet."

The sergeant nodded, took a deep breath, and tapped his pen on the kitchen table. It was some seconds before he sighed again and made some more notes.

******

The shooting took top billing on the television news that evening. It started at the Police Media and Public Affairs Branch. The spokesperson, in the usual taciturn manner of the force, would only say they were following a certain line of enquiry. The coverage switched quickly to the facade of Laurie Lyall's house. The focus zoomed in on the boarded-up window and door. It provided a dramatic backdrop for a young male reporter to speak to camera and reveal what the police had not; they were investigating a possible connection between the attack on the house and the occupant's involvement in the recent protest against the proposed Sleighmen development. Laurie Lyall, however, kept a low profile and refused to appear on-camera. The camera operator panned across the pockmarked walls of the house for a few seconds, as the reporter segued into a crossover.

Outside the main entrance to Keeala Resort, a female reporter brushed a wisp of hair from her face, nodded to her camera operator and counted down; three – two – one. An eclectic scrum of bodies jostled for position behind her. Members of CARP, perhaps twenty strong, were easy to pick out as they held their banners and signs above their heads. The members of Lyall's group showed how well practised they were in the art of protest, as they muscled their way through to the front of the crowd. They made sure their placards faced the cameras as they chanted the protester's hymn, "What do we want – no development – When don't we want it – now – What do we want ... " Placards and banners waved, proclaiming *CARP - Campaign Against the Rape of the Planet*, and others urging *Stop the dodgy developer* and *No Development Here*.

Whilst their appearance and demeanour distinguished the resort residents and neighbouring property owners from Lyall's mob, they too, despite their differing motives, wanted a chance to air their grievances to the thousands of viewers.

The reporter held a microphone close to her lips and said, as she turned to a man beside her, "And you, sir, why are you here?" She pointed a microphone at an older man, smartly dressed in cream slacks and navy jacket.

He stood tall and straight, a silver moustache emphasising his distinguished bearing; ex-military, perhaps.

He had pushed his way determinedly through the CARP crush to the front of the crowd, where he had then elbowed aside a rough looking man chanting the protesters' mantra.

"We're not happy about this proposed development, at all," he said. He spoke confidently, with an air of authority. He looked straight into the lens. "Some of us paid substantial premiums to secure our sites because of their uninterrupted views. We look across the lake to the bushland on the far shore and the mountains behind. Not only will we lose those views if the proposed expansion takes place, but we'll be looking straight into other people's homes – and vice versa. Moreover, it's not just the loss of amenity that concerns us. Many of us have invested our life savings in our homes here. If this development goes ahead, the value of our investment will most surely go down. While most of us will leave this place in a pine box and won't be worried for ourselves, it's not fair that our beneficiaries should lose out."

Cheers erupted and *Leave our resort alone!* Placards in the rear ranks of the crowd attracted the TV camera operator's attention.

A man, probably late thirtyish, had come through the crowd in the older man's wake. He raised a hand and looked at the reporter. She held out the microphone to him and gave him a nod.

He cleared his throat and said, "My family, and many others like us, live out here for the peace and quiet. We don't want all the extra traffic and noise that this development will bring. There'll be parties and noise at all hours of the day and night. Our kids won't be safe on the roads with these half-blind geriatrics weaving all over the roads – there'll be no peace if this goes ahead. Our lifestyles will be ruined." The hypocrisy and exaggeration that flowed from this speaker's mouth was lost in a chorus of cheers.

Latent in all communities, the NIMBY syndrome now had a chance to fester and spread amongst Keeala Resort's neighbours. The 'Not In My Backyard' fever fuelled the disquiet and ensured the facts relating to the development became more and more distorted, fed by rumour and deliberate mistruths. Illogical as most of their objections were to this proposed development, the surrounding property owners were ready for a fight with Keeala Resort's owners, despite being in denial about their supposedly quiet rural lifestyle.

Trouble was brewing for the owners of Keeala Resort – on more than one front.

******

Two men, one much older, stood staring at the television screen on the wall of a small, cluttered office. The volume was low but the vision was telling the story.

"You know what really gives me the shits with all this, Andrew?" The older man waved a hand at the screen. "These people who object – look at them – well many of them anyway, they're just professional bloody rabble-rousers. Christ, I mingled in the crowd at a protest against Dick Manner's development a few weeks ago. You know the place?"

"I haven't been there but it's down on the south-side, isn't it?"

"Yeah, well over an hour from Keeala Resort, way down on the south side of Brisbane, Gold Coast in fact, but I'd reckon half the bloody faces I saw there were the same ones we're looking at here. You can't tell me all these people are simply locals objecting to us as a local issue. They're bloody rent-a-mob most of them, bloody layabouts, under achievers, jealous of anyone who has the brains to make money. Who do they think pays the taxes to send them their fortnightly stay-at-home money? I'll bet half of them don't even know what they're protesting about. I hate the pricks."

Andrew Sleighmen said to his father, Roger. "Well, Laurie Lyall's the one I'm worried about. He looks like he's going to be more of a problem than we anticipated. I thought he would've been in no doubt about the message we sent him this morning. I know there was no sign of him on TV but I thought he had a few more brains than most of this lot. If that's true though, how come his mob appeared out of the woodwork so damned quick this afternoon? He has to be behind it, surely?"

"Maybe, but look, son, some of these greenie bastards actually think they're on a mission from God to save the planet. Lyall's one of them and he's certainly no dummy, that's for sure, but some of his lefty mates are just as committed." His hands waved at the TV again. "Just look at what's going on here with these half-wits, and that's after we've just given Lyall what should've been the fright of his life. You'd think the others would've been smart enough to get the message, wouldn't you?"

Andrew nodded but said nothing. He had an idea what was coming.

His father continued, " Look, let's give him the benefit of the doubt for the time being and assume his lieutenants organised this crap, but, by Christ, if he did organise this and thinks he can just stay out of sight but still direct his CARP mob, he's got another thing coming. He's got the strength of his convictions, Andrew, and that's what makes him so bloody dangerous to us. He's cunning and single-minded, but if he's not brought to heel he could cost us a lot of money, son, a bloody lot of money." Spittle flew from the corners of Roger's mouth. His face reddened and he started shouting, "I haven't finished with him, not by a long shot. I bloody well won't let him get in my way; him, or his ratbag followers and I shouldn't have to remind you, mate, that I made Laurie Lyall your responsibility." Roger Sleighmen was panting. Sweat rolled off his florid face. He slumped into a chair.

"I'll take care of him, don't you worry about that."

"But I do worry, Andrew, I do worry. I'm starting to think that if I want something done I have to bloody well do it myself." Roger Sleighmen was gasping. He caught his breath for a couple of seconds. "Shit, mate, I brought you into this business to help me, not to be a liability. You've got to get this Lyall bastard sorted out. Get me a bloody cup of coffee, will you – and my friggin' cigarettes – and be quick about it."

Andrew clenched his teeth and struggled to keep the back answer to himself. This was not the first time his father had spoken to him like this, but each time it happened Andrew's resentment grew stronger. He was glad for the diversion of the coffee making but, as he walked to the kitchenette, he had the feeling the tirade would continue.

After a couple of minutes, the senior Sleighmen got up from his chair and went to the open door of the kitchenette. He stuck his head in and yelled at Andrew, "What the hell are you doing in there? Jesus, I could've boiled water quicker by rubbing two sticks together. And where's my cigarettes?"

Andrew reached over, picked up a near empty pack from the top of a small refrigerator, and handed it to his father.

"Well?"

"Well what?"

"Well, what am I supposed to light it with – a bloody bolt of lightning?"

It took all the control he could muster for Andrew not to respond. He knew if he replied he would not be able to trust himself not to tell his father how he really felt about him. He grabbed a lighter from the kitchen bench and thrust it at his father without making eye contact.

Sleighmen Snr. let the gesture go unchallenged but continued with his diatribe. "Look, you've got to get on top of this Lyall bastard. I don't want all the work, not to mention all the money I've put into the councillors, to be for naught because they get nervous about Lyall stirring up resentment with the voters." Roger paused to draw breath, and then continued. "And there's another thing, if I may be so bold as to ask. What the flamin' hell is going on with the landholders? We can't build these units in the bloody thin air, can we?" He tapped a cigarette out of the packet and lit it as he returned to his chair. He took a drag and coughed violently.

Andrew came out of the kitchenette and placed a cup of coffee on top of a small filing cabinet beside his father's chair. Without stopping, he continued to the front door of the office.

"I'm going out. We're short of coffee," he said, as he walked off.

There was no reply from his father as he left. Andrew doubted his father could hear him above the almost non-stop hacking and wheezing, nor did he care. All he wanted was to get out of his father's presence and clear his head.

******

Not far from the office was a small park. Andrew found a seat in a quiet corner and sat down. He clasped his hands behind his head and stretched his body as he let out a slow breath, trying to relax. For a few seconds he stayed in that position, then sat upright, placed his hands on his thighs, closed his eyes and began a meditation technique he had learnt at a Yoga course. He tried to clear his awareness of the outside world and to see, in his mind's eye, a never-ending spiral of light that would concentrate his focus on the infinite hole at the centre. He would exclude all external stimuli from rational examination; sounds, smells, the breeze on his face, would be noted but paid no attention – or so the theory of the practice went.

"Damn," said Andrew, after a couple of minutes of trying. He usually had little trouble slipping into the routine, but today he was so affected by his father's gibes he knew it would be a struggle.

******

As Andrew sat, he started to brood over his situation. He thought how his father had become a self-made man, overcoming the handicap of a minimum education to drag himself out of his family's working class background. Andrew did admire his father's drive and ambition. They were traits that had helped his father become the owner of one of the largest chains of retirement villages and Over 50's resorts in Australia but, no matter how Andrew tried to rationalise his father's achievements, he knew that drive and ambition alone had not been the only factors in his success. His father had always been reticent about the details, but

Andrew knew corruption, coercion, and intimidation were often part of his father's deals.

Andrew's mind continued to churn. He remembered the time, soon after he had joined the business, when he had come across some documents on his father's desk. One page of double-spaced writing, titled 'Feasibility Study', had an account attached for $10,000. When Andrew read the report he realised it was virtually worthless, its contents being little more than a few paragraphs of business-speak and a conclusion that a certain project would be viable. When he had queried the value of that report with his father, he had told Andrew that certain palms had to be greased to achieve positive outcomes for the business, and paying for dummy reports was just one way to disguise the money that changed hands. At that time, Andrew accepted his father's justification that that was how many businesses operated and that such *expenses* were just treated as overheads and the payments were simply passed on to the consumer.

Andrew could not deny how much he had benefited materially from being Roger Sleighmen's son but, as he sat on that bench, he started to wonder whether he wanted to continue paying the price for that privilege. His father's constant criticism and sarcastic comments disturbed Andrew, but something much more worrying, more fundamental, nagged at his conscience. Roger Sleighmen was a crook – and Andrew had become his accomplice.

******

Frightening off the protesters was Andrew's job and he had already taken the first step in that direction. The attack on Laurie Lyall's house had been Andrew's responsibility. Three weeks before the shooting incident, Andrew had found himself in a bar talking to a Karl Simmens, a moustachioed but otherwise bald, rent-a-muscle, fix-it man. Andrew explained what was required and how much he was prepared to pay. Simmens played a hard hand and laughed at Andrew's first offer. Andrew feigned shock at Simmens' refusal and said he could go no higher. Silence ensued as the two stared at each other. Andrew spoke first and said he would make a phone call. A smirk crossed Simmens' face as he watched Andrew pick up his phone and move a couple of seats away, but not quite out of his hearing. Andrew dialled his office fax number and spoke to the fax call tones as they beeped in his ear. Andrew held his hand over his mobile phone and pressed it close to his ear to mask the high-pitched fax tone, as it continued its part in the charade.

"Hi." ... "No, he won't take it." ... "Says it's an insult." ... "No, says double." ... "Out of the question?" ... "Right, yeah. I understand."

Andrew sat next to Simmens again. "No, Simmens, double is just not on. However, we are prepared to meet you half way – and that, I can assure you, will be our final offer."

Simmens stroked his bushy lip as he considered the proposition. "Ah, I don't know, mate. You understand I won't be doing the job myself? I'll be sub-contracting, you might say, leaving it to the specialists. Lots of mouths to feed, you know?"

"Take it, or leave it."

More moustache stroking followed until, "Aaargh, I wouldn't normally cut my rates for anyone, but let's call it a goodwill gesture, repeat client and all that. You're on." Simmens looked unhappy as he had shaken hands with

Andrew, but he was smiling on the inside. He had scored $2,000 more than he had expected.

"Done," said Andrew, as he released his grasp on Simmens' hand. Andrew felt a surge of elation but kept a poker face. He could not stop thinking how pleased his father would be when he told him how he had managed to get Simmens to accept $5,000 less than they had been prepared to pay.

The seriousness of what Andrew had just done had not then registered in his conscience.

******

Roger Sleighmen was a big man in many ways - stature and gut, ambition and determination. His hair was white and hung thinly over his forehead. Though expensive, his clothes always looked untidy. His shirts were invariably ill fitting and he scuffed along in his loafers with a swagger that was all such an obese man could manage. Roger had many associates, but few friends. His occasional mistresses could not be called friends; employees would be a better description. He was not the least bit sentimental and had little patience for anyone who was. He was a man whose life, ever since his teenage years, had been driven by the all-consuming desire to make money.

"I'll stop when I'm dead," he had once told Andrew.

Whenever he looked at his father now, Andrew wondered if that might be sooner rather than later. Roger was a chain smoker and was rarely without his incessant cough. He regularly swallowed antibiotics for chest infections and he ate all the wrong foods. In the past, Andrew had tried to encourage his father to do regular exercise and eat a healthy diet, but Roger had made it abundantly clear he wanted no advice about how he should live his life, so Andrew desisted.

In contrast, Andrew saw himself as a healthy young man who spent at least an hour, five days a week, maintaining his fitness, much to his father's disgust. Roger told Andrew so often that exercise was a waste of time, that Andrew finally told him he too, did not need advice.

Andrew grew up listening to his father's opinions on everything from food to politics. He idolised his father when he was younger and he inherited some of his father's arrogance. Andrew never overcame the sense of loss that came from never having known his mother. His father cast her adrift when Andrew was very young. Andrew inherited his mother's Irish good looks, pale skin, and dark hair. He fancied he also had her disposition and pragmatic view of life, having heard this description of her from his grandparents when he was young. He knew his impression of the world around him was formed largely through his father's influence but, as he got older, he found he could make his own judgements and form his personal opinions, despite his father's disapproval. He too was ambitious, but not as needy as Roger, who had started life with nothing. He never knew what it was to be poor, as his father had done.

The Sleighmen Group, a privately owned company, had a string of Over 50's resorts and retirement villages throughout Australia. The company had enough financial security to undertake at least one more stage at Keeala Resort, close to the outskirts of Brisbane. Roger Sleighmen, the founder and Managing Director, wanted to take advantage of the ever-increasing demand for his product. Approval for another sixty homes was his goal but the biggest obstacle, apart from his battle with the anti-everything mob, as he called them, was securing enough land. That also, was Andrew's responsibility.

******

Joe Monteno was a wiry little farmer with thinning hair and a big nose. He and his wife owned the largest property on the other side of the lake. They operated a genuine business, a market garden, which supplied some of the few remaining independent fruit and vegetable businesses in the area. His wife, Beryl, had complained to him on more than one occasion that he was almost seventy and could not continue his physically demanding occupation much longer. When the first stage of Keeala Resort was built, she expressed an interest in a home there but her husband dismissed the idea at the time and said he was not ready to turn into a bowls-playing, community-singing geriatric. Mrs. Monteno was delighted then, when a representative of the Sleighmen Group recently approached them with a view to purchasing their land for the proposed expansion. She was even more excited when her husband unexpectedly agreed it might be time to take it a bit easier.

******

"Trouble is, they want it for almost nothing," whinged Joe to Karl Simmens, as they sat at a table in a quiet corner of the local pub. Andrew Sleighmen was the person who approached the Montenos but, despite having made what Andrew considered a fair offer, they could not agree on a price. Andrew mentioned the problem to Karl Simmens when he was organising the Laurie Lyall business. The remark had been little more than a conversation filler at the time and Andrew was surprised when Simmens immediately said he might have a solution, not only to the purchase of the Monteno's land , but the other parcels as well. He said he had been able to help a politician in New South Wales who had faced a similar problem.

"Joe," said Simmens, "I think I can solve your problem about the price. Let's say you scratch my back and I'll scratch yours, you know what I mean? And let's say that you help us to convince your neighbours that it would be in their best interests to sell. Now, if that happens, you and your wife will be very, very happy, I assure you."

"So, what's the deal?"

Simmens moved his chair closer to Joe and made a show of looking around the room slowly, before resting his elbow on the table and cupping his hand over his mouth. "Well, here's what I have in mind. Let us say there used to be a cattle dip on your property and you are concerned arsenic and other nasty chemicals, like maybe DDT, may have contaminated your soil. You're located on the highest ground around the lake and when it rains the run off flows across the neighbouring properties, right?" Karl produced a topographical map from his coat pocket and spread it on the table. "See how this gully intersects all the properties we're interested in?"

"Sure, but how could I explain not having known about the dip?"

"Easy. Your family were the original settlers in this area, weren't they, what, three generation ago? All you have to say is that you came across a trunk in the loft of your shed recently and it contained some very old documents. One of those referred to the disused dip."

"Yeah, but there was no dip and a simple soil test will come up negative for contamination," Joe jumped in.

Karl put his hand up, "Hang on, hang on, and hear me out. Have you ever heard of salting a gold mine? Same principle here. It'd be easy enough to spread a little arsenic around, wouldn't it, if we had to? Anyhow, it more than likely will never get to that stage. All you need to do is start the rumour. You tell one of your neighbours, in confidence, of course. That's the best way to ensure it spreads. When you start a rumour, it's hard to find out where it began. Keeping a lid on a secret is impossible once it starts to spread and, the more you deny something, the more people believe it."

Joe nodded and began to follow Karl's train of thought. "So, if I was to say, to the right person, that I may be selling out because I'm worried about chemical contamination affecting my land, and then later deny I ever said it, that could start speculation and cause others to consider their options, and so on and so on."

Karl smiled with both lips squeezed together, then said, "Exactly. If we have to, we can arrange soil tests to reflect whatever result we have in mind. Understand?" Karl leaned toward Joe and smiled sarcastically.

Jo had the feeling Karl was losing patience with him.

"Yeah, I know where I stand, now that you've spelt it out. I'll have to square Beryl away so she keeps her mouth shut. My wife likes the good things in life but not always the price you have to pay, but don't worry, I know what I have to do."

******

19

"I do believe that first impressions mean a great deal, no matter what you say, son. I've been in this bloody game long enough to know what I'm talking about, for Christ's sake."

"Look, I acknowledge your experience, Dad, but in this case I think giving the new development a different name is not a good move. We've already built up a good reputation with the existing project and the name, 'Keeala Resort', has the connotation of a quality, up-market lifestyle. It's a trusted brand in the community and I really don't agree with you about a name change. Look, if you want to dismiss everything I say, fine, but if you must change the name I really feel we should capitalise on the goodwill of the Keeala brand when we build Stage 4."

"What do you mean?" Roger Sleighmen swivelled around in his chair to face his son, a scowl flashing across his face.

"Well, what about Keeala Terraces or Keeala Gardens?" Andrew lifted his palms upward to suggest the possibilities were endless. "At least that way we would still get *some* spin-off from the Keeala name."

"Argh, is that the sort of shit they taught you in that pooncie marketing course. Bloody academics, wouldn't know a self-made dollar if it bit 'em on the arse. Let's take another look at those plans. We'll sort out the bloody name later."

They walked over to a large table in their office where the expansion plans for Keeala Resort lay. They stood together, one gross and untidy, the other handsome and fit, and looked down at the current plans for this latest project.

"I like the idea that these new homes are going to be so much more prestigious than the others. I don't think we'll have any problems disposing of them," Roger said to his son.

"We got two more expressions of interest yesterday. That's taken us over the half way mark already. I'm beginning to think we should have been catering to this market from the start," Andrew ventured. "Not only are they easier to sell, but there's a better margin as well."

"Yeah, there's good money in them, but it's all in theory isn't it, until we get contracts on those land parcels. Oh, by the way, have the managers agreed to stay on, or are we going to be looking for new blood?" Roger threw the question over his shoulder to Andrew as he walked to the drinks cabinet, discreetly hidden by a partition in a corner of the office.

Chapter Two

Di Watersen leaned over the balcony of the manager's residence at Keeala Resort and waved to her husband, Jim.

"I'm up here."

He looked up from the driveway and acknowledged her wave with a smile.

"I'll be right up." He ran into the house and took the stairs, two at a time. "Hi," he puffed, as he arrived on the balcony and put his arms around his wife's waist.

"And *Hi* to you, too," said Di, with a hint of exasperation as she felt his laboured breaths on the back of her neck. She turned within his encircling arms and stared into his eyes for a few seconds. She sighed and said, "Oh, Jim, I wish you'd take your doctor's advice seriously. You know what he said about exerting yourself. Look, I'm not trying to be a nag, honestly, but I don't want to be a widow at my age. I want to have a long and happy old age – with you."

"Yeah, yeah," said Jim. He released his grip on her as he fought to control his breathing. "Phew ... yeah ... you're absolutely right, as usual. It was a silly thing to do."

"Well, the last thing you need is another heart attack. We both know you've had your warning, The next one might be more serious, but anyhow, I won't labour the point," said Di.

She pointed to a small, wrought-iron table. A small bowl of beer nuts, two champagne flutes and an ice bucket with an opened bottle waited.

"It's your favourite, Sparkling Shiraz," said Di. Her face softened into a smile. It turned into a fleeting kiss.

"Boy, I'm sure looking forward to a drink," he said, as he pulled out a chair for Di. "You've no idea how much stuff I've got through today. Those last managers certainly left things in a mess."

Jim took the other chair and gazed at his wife. His expression rarely failed to soften when he laid eyes on his wife of almost ten years. As he looked at her, he realised he was still attracted to her delicate facial features and her soft, long hair that always escaped the twist wound at the back of her head. Her slim, agile body was constantly on the move and Jim had yet to tire of watching her hips sway in what he thought was a sensuous, yet innocent display. Physical attractions aside, Jim knew that the real glue which bound them, now they were in their fifties, was that each really appreciated having a partner with whom they resonated. As Jim continued to stare, he became acutely aware of the immense joy and companionship they brought into each other's life.

"Penny for your thoughts," said Di, as she clicked her fingers in front of Jim's face.

"Oh, sorry, darling – was a thousand miles away. How've you been getting along?"

"Oh, still trying to unpack in between all the interruptions. Seems like I've answered the phone and the front door about a million times. Anyone would think they'd never had new managers here before." Di sipped her drink and looked back at Jim, the fingers of her left hand tapping gently on the tabletop.

Jim smiled and placed his hand over hers. He caressed her fingers. He thought how Di would be worried he would be pushing himself to the limit, as usual, and he could understand her concern about his running up the stairs. Jim thought how Di often, and with sincerity, told him he looked more distinguished with each passing day, but Jim realised he was not just beginning to show his age, with his silvery hair and deep laugh lines around his eyes and mouth, but he was starting to feel it.

The past two weeks had been difficult for the residents and relief manager. The previous managers had left without notice and Di and Jim had stepped in to fill the vacuum. The resort owner knew them to be reliable and trustworthy and appreciated their skills; Jim's background was in business and real estate management and Di's as a registered nurse. They complemented one another and ran a tight ship. They had hoped to hold out for a less stressful situation than the one that loomed ahead now. As usual though, they took it in their stride.

Chapter Three

Almost forty and very fit, Laurie Lyall was the epitome of a good dad, husband and employee. He was a vegetarian and a zealous environmentalist. Highly motivated and energetic, he was a man with causes to conquer, but right now, his problem was placating his wife.

"Look, love, I can't take a day off work every time you get stressed out. The police have things in hand and I doubt those mugs will try anything like that again. I'm sure they'll leave it at that." Determined to hide his distress, Laurie tried to avoid adding to the emotion of the situation.

Marian sounded furious. "So here we stay, like sitting ducks, waiting for the next attack on our children and our home."

"That's pretty unlikely. The police say that whoever was responsible for the attack was making a point and now they've done it. They were trying to scare us off. Me, that is."

"Well, they've certainly scared me off. I'm going to stay with Dad. I can't take chances with our children's lives. You do what you like." Marian pushed her long hair back from her face; she looked tired and older than her thirty-five years.

"Marian, please? I agree the risks are too great. I'm backing out, as of today. I remember when the first stage of the resort was being built, and Jon Chamberlaine took a major role in the protest. He eventually disappeared, no one knows where, but obviously someone scared him off in the same way they are trying intimidate me now. I assure you, there'll be no more caring about the environment or corrupt developers. I'm finished with the lot, I promise! I handed in my resignation to the group this afternoon." His voice was pleading as he walked toward his wife with his arms out.

"Well that may be, but I still don't feel safe staying here, Laurie. Whoever did this to us wouldn't know you've resigned and they could be back. These people obviously put no value on human life, and have no concern for the effects of today's attack on the kids, or me. What if the kids, or you, me, any of us, had been sitting at the dining room table behind the French doors, eh? Have you thought of that?"

Marian turned back to her packing with tears in her eyes. She had made it clear that she loved the way Laurie had stood up for what he believed in and she had been so proud of him when she saw the respect he engendered in others, but now, she could see that his ideals fell away to insignificance when tested against the lives of their family. She burst into tears, turned and walked into Laurie's arms, eager for the comfort and security of his love.

He held her close. "Things are very quiet with the computer repairs. Maybe we can have a little holiday. What if I ring the boss? I think he would be agreeable to my taking a week or so off. He's never agreed with my views, especially about development, but if I tell him I've quit the organization I think he'll come to the party."

Marian nodded and watched while her husband rang his boss and organised for them to disappear for two weeks. He turned to her and said "Surely, in a few weeks, things will have cooled off and maybe even be resolved."

******

Joe Monteno pushed his cap back and scratched his head in thought, as he drove home from his meeting with Karl. He could see how it all could work and he began to formulate a plan. He would begin with Reg, his old friend and neighbour of the past forty years. He would tell Reg, in confidence of course, about a few problems he'd been having for a long time that he had never mentioned before. Up until now, he would say, he had kept it to himself, but now that someone was showing an interest in buying his property, he was going to snap up the offer. He would say nothing to the buyer about the soil problems affecting his crops and his cattle. For a man, Reg was a good talker, even a better gossip than Beryl. Joe knew that his *confidential* talk with Reg would soon be a topic for discussion among the other neighbours. Later, just to make sure, he would tell Beryl exactly what he wanted to have broadcast. The less she knew about the facts, the better chance of success. Joe smiled to himself; the possibilities were endless and he was already enjoying the ideas that were popping into his head. Karl had suggested that a nice high-rise unit on the Gold Coast already had his name on it, if they were able to secure all the properties the Sleighmens had earmarked. Joe could visualise his retirement unit with sweeping views across the glitter strip of Surfers Paradise to the ocean and yes, maybe he would take up golf. This was his one big chance and he was not prepared to let it slip through his fingers.

******

Westbridge City Council Mayor, Colin Porterman, stepped up to the lectern and looked across at the faces waiting for him to begin. He realised he would really miss this job if he was not re-elected at the polls in March of the next year. Still, after four years, he had had a good run, made lots of money and friends and had influence in all sorts of places. He wondered how much that would change if he was not the Mayor. He was not so naive as to believe many people liked him only for himself, but he figured he would always have some influence. He knew a lot of big business secrets, and he still had a few favours owing.

Only yesterday, Council had approved a big high-rise development, previously rejected, but now resubmitted. A well-orchestrated campaign by the Greens and a strong, ultra-radical activist group called CARP had been responsible for the initial rejection. Porterman smiled as he thought about the acronym, CARP - Campaign Against the Rape of the Planet.

Mayor Porterman had, only last week, accepted a gift from a thankful developer. This gift of money, which he would share with certain other councillors, was in response to the promised passage of the approvals to build that particular high rise on land that had previously been set aside for parkland. With a few minor changes, such as a little more open space and a few more parking spaces, the developers in question would soon begin the project, despite previous objections by CARP.

News of the high-rise approval greeted Laurie when he arrived home following his two weeks in Cairns with his family. He sat staring at the newspaper article with incredulity. He and his fellow protesters had worked so hard to ensure that particular development would not be passed. *Bastards*, Laurie thought.

The phone rang. "Hi, Laurie, have you seen the news?" It was Peter Dawson, a founding member of CARP.

"Mate, I'm just this minute reading it. I'm absolutely disgusted, angry, and frustrated. How the hell did those mongrels get their plans passed after all the irrefutable evidence we prepared for the council. I thought that whole deal was dead in the water last year. And now, how could they have possibly satisfied the council with what they now know about the damage to the environment, particularly the water contamination problems?"

"I know, I know. I absolutely agree and feeling is running pretty high here right now. There are a couple of members here talking terrorism to stop the project. I'm sure they aren't serious but they're awfully upset."

"You know I resigned from CARP a couple of weeks ago?"

"Yeah, I heard, but I don't believe it. Are you really leaving us?"

Laurie sighed. "I had no choice after the attack on the family. Unless I want to be a single man, I have to let go of my involvement."

"Real sorry to hear that, mate. Listen; can I talk to you, maybe later this evening? I have a few ideas I want to put to you, sort of on the quiet."

"I won't change my mind, Peter, if that's what it's about. I've made a promise to Marian and I can't continue when my family is threatened."

"Sure, I agree. No, this is something else. I can't talk now. It needs to be in person. How about I meet you at the library? It's late-closing, say 7.30?" suggested Peter.

Laurie hesitated but finally agreed to the meeting. He sat pensively as Marian ran back and forth unpacking the bags and muttering to herself.

Laurie's feelings for the protest group ran deep and he had been a member since its inception more than five years previously. He knew he could not sit by and watch his hard work undone, but what else was open to him? He stood up, "What can I do to help? Are all the bags in?"

"Well, let's hope I haven't left any work for you, dear!" Marian put her head down, wiped the sweat from her face, and walked away.

******

Laurie met with Peter Dawson just before 7.30 that evening.

"You're looking well, mate – must have needed that break," said Peter.

They shook hands and walked toward a small lounge at the back of the municipal library. They were both grateful for the air conditioning.

"So what's up?" Laurie asked Peter. They had known one another for years and had no need of formalities.

"I've been giving a lot of thought to the situation with our friendly local council. Most of them are doing well but one wonders how some of them can live quite as well as they do, considering their so-called, modest income."

Laurie looked intently at his friend and was interested now. Peter was talking about a subject close to Laurie's heart;

corruption among some of the members of the council. They had discussed this many times, but no one had a solution.

Peter said, "Laurie, you know the old saying, 'If you can't beat 'em, join 'em'. What do you think about that?"

"Keep talking."

"Well, what we need is a man on the inside – on the Council."

"You mean me?"

"I do."

"Ah, look, I've considered it before, but the thought of sitting in a room with that bunch of crooks doesn't turn me on."

"Yeah, I know, mate, I can understand that, but this is for a higher cause, and you wouldn't be without support – a lot of support – but it would have to be, sort of, undercover. Know what I mean?"

"Sure, but I can see so many obstacles already. To begin with, there's Marian. In all conscience, Peter, I couldn't have Marian and the kids subjected again to anything like the fear that shooting put into the family. I really do have to think about the danger I might be exposing the family to, and another thing, I enjoy my job and I don't want to lose it. I know I'd be better off financially in the short term, but sometimes money isn't everything. Don't forget too, even if I did get elected this time, there's no guarantee I'd get in next time. I'd be four years older and out looking for a job again and there're lots of young kids churning out of TAFEs and Unis looking to break into IT and computers."

"Laurie, you're already more than qualified for the job. There's enough time to prepare a campaign strategy, and CARP would support you, both physically and financially. Of course, an election account would be set up and all donations disclosed. You know the nomination procedure, I'm sure, and you'd get all the advice you need as to how to run the campaign. Just think, you'd have four years to get in there and have influence in decision making about so many causes that have been dear to you for a very long time. You could make a difference! You could really change things for the better."

"Yeah, but just listen to yourself, mate. I think maybe you would be a better man for the job."

"No, no, no, Laurie! We all know you're the one with the charisma, the gift of the gab, and the ability to sway an audience. I've seen you in action, mate. You're the man for us!"

"So, you have discussed this with the executive?"

"I have, and we all agreed. After losing Jon Chamberlaine a few years ago, no one has been able to fill his shoes, until you, now. You're smarter than Jon is as well. He was a great talker, but he wasn't as politically savvy as you, my friend." Peter took a deep breath and opened his mouth to continue. Laurie put up his hand.

"Hang on, Pete. Do you want me to represent CARP, or run as an independent?"

"We all agree you should run as an independent. That way, you'll be able to use preferences where you like, and we trust your integrity to stand up for the issues that have always been important to us. There are the loose alliances in council, as we know, and you will have the independence and freedom of your own conscience. We have a great deal of confidence in you Laurie. There is no one we trust more."

"I'm going to need a little time to think about this, Peter. I have to admit the idea excites me and I really am not yet ready to hang up my banner. However, I'll need Marian onside and that's my first and major obstacle. Give us a couple of days to think it over, eh?" Laurie pursed his lips and nodded his head He was already deep in thought about the differences this sort of a change would bring to his life.

Chapter Four

Beryl slammed the shopping bags down on the kitchen bench and looked for her husband.

"Where the hell are you, you stupid man?"

She found him in the laundry, scrubbing his hands.

"What's all the noise about?"

He looked over his shoulder at his wife and saw she was not happy.

"I met Marjorie Wilson at the supermarket just now, and guess what she told me."

"I give up. What did that old cow have to say?"

They both walked out to the veranda and sat down.

"She said that poison from the old dip site has travelled down the creek and contaminated everyone's property. Now our property isn't worth a pinch of shit and no one will buy it. We'll all be stuck with land that's unusable and unsellable."

Joe whistled. "That sounds pretty serious. How did fat Marjorie know-it-all find out about this?"

"Apparently, it's pretty much common knowledge with all the neighbours. We're always the last to know, of course." Beryl huffed and got up to walk back to the kitchen.

"Yeah, ain't that the truth," he said.

Joe could not wipe the smile off his face.

"All going to plan," he said to Beryl's back.

******

And everything was going to plan. Karl Simmens had been busy, as had Joe. The rumour was out now. Andrew Sleighmen's sales representative approached the local landowners and made offers for their land, subject to council approval of course. Two were agreeable, one was holding out for a better offer, and one point-blank refused all offers.

Council required soil and water tests to accompany the development plan, along with many other studies and recommendations. They would be independent studies and they would be 'clean', as planned. By that time, most of the local landowners would be happy to move on. They would be glad the authorities did not find out about the 'so called' contamination that had been whispered about, in the weeks prior to their sale.

"I feel confident that the couple holding out will cave-in before we go to council," said Karl to Andrew, a week before they submitted their plan.

They agreed that 'sweeteners' might be offered if they were running out of time and still had not reached their goal. The developers knew this process well and they knew they had majority support in the council.

******

"We don't expect any problems with the land owners, Dad. Have you made contact with your friends on the council?" Andrew asked his father.

"I have and it seems the price of sitting on your arse and voting yes is getting more expensive every year. I'm beginning to think we may need some new blood in council; someone a little more appreciative of who paid to get him there."

"There are elections coming up in March. Do you want to do anything about it before then?"

"No time, but I think it is time our friends on council felt a little less comfortable. I'm not paying them for nothing, eh?" A sly grin crossed his face as he said it.

******

"You still awake?" Marian asked, as she turned to Laurie in bed, reached out gently, and touched his shoulder.

"Hmm. Can't sleep again. I can't stop thinking. My brain won't switch off."

"What's the trouble? Is it work?"

"No. Well, it could be, if I decide to do it."

"What do you mean?"

"I was planning to talk to you about it in the morning." Laurie reached over, switched on the bedside lamp, and wriggled into a sitting position. He looked down at his wife and decided to deal with the issue. "I guess now is as good a time as any. I've been asked to nominate for local council, in March this year."

For a moment, Laurie could almost hear his wife digesting his words. "So you'd be a full-time councillor?"

"If I'm elected, yes. The money's better than what I get now and you'd have a busier social life."

"So whose party would you be on, the Greens?"

Laurie shook his head. "No, I'd be running as an independent. I'd be my own man. You know my agenda, where my interest lies. I'd have an opportunity to address some of the issues that are important to me."

"These people, do they have anything to do with CARP?"

"Some of them."

"So, they're the ones who approached you. Would they be paying for your campaign?"

"Some of them." Laurie felt Marian stiffen. She sat up and turned to look at him.

"What are you telling me? Would you be a council member with the intention of pursuing all the same issues that you did with the group?"

"No, I would vote strictly based on the facts presented and my own conscience."

"And we all know where that lies." She slipped down between the sheets again and turned her back to her husband. She sighed, sniffed and shook her head. "This could still be a dangerous occupation, couldn't it?"

"Any occupation can be dangerous. I could be a truck driver or a postman; I could get run over on the way to work."

"Computer repairmen rarely get killed in the course of their work." Silence followed.

"I'm going to run at the end of March. I've made up my mind and I hope before then you'll come to agree with that it's the right decision – for me. I can't hide from the things I believe in. I can't try to remain safe at all costs. I have to fulfil my potential and do what I know is right. I hope one day you'll be proud of my decision."

"Yeah, I'm sure the kids and I will be very proud of you at your graveside. That's if they don't get us too!" Marian got up and walked to the small guest room opposite their bedroom. She slammed the door.

Laurie sighed. He suspected this would be his wife's response, but it did not change his mind.

******

Marian lay and stared at the ceiling as she allowed her anger to abate. She began to think about the time she first met Laurie and was not surprised that this situation had finally arisen. Before they had married, she and Laurie often attended rallies and protests in support of the issues they felt strongly about. They worked as Red Cross volunteers in their gap year, before they started at university. She remembered how they agreed not to have children until they were over thirty. That made her laugh; she became pregnant a few weeks after their wedding and her university education went on hold while Laurie worked part time and studied computer engineering the rest of the time. Her children became her career and she worked at it equally as hard as her husband did his.

My children need their dad and I need my soul mate. Somehow, we have to get though this, together. Marian held that thought as she got up and went back to the bed where Laurie lay, also staring at the ceiling. He threw the sheet back and Marian slid in next to him. He put both his arms around her and held her close.

"I don't want to die knowing I was only ever motivated by trying to remain safe," he said. "Neither of us ever had that as a priority and our children will have to learn it as well. As long as they are around us they'll have to be brave enough to stand up for what they believe in and not be intimidated by bullies. That's what I think anyway."

Marian looked at Laurie and smiled

Laurie put his face against his wife's hair and breathed in the smell of the woman who had never let him down. They were going to work together to make a better world for their children – if only in a very small way.

Chapter Five

Jim looked up at the man knocking on his open door. The office was open, and Jim had managed to clear away all the seriously urgent business and now sat at his desk, scrolling down a web page on his computer.

"Come in," he said, and smiled at the dapper looking man who came toward him and extended his hand.

"I'm Robert Wieland. Harold, my partner, and I live in Unit 36. We're in the group of three-bedroom homes, on the right."

They shook hands across the desk. "How are you, Robert? Nice to meet you. I'm Jim Watersen. Take a seat."

"I'm sure you're busy, Jim, but I wanted to tell you how happy we all are to see you and your good wife settle in. This is a great place to live and I think you'll find that out yourself. Nothing too dramatic happens around here, and that's the way we like it. They're a great bunch of people, most enjoying a content retirement. A few misfits, as everywhere, and a few still go to work – a few mugs!" Robert laughed at his own joke. "But, they all fit in and we have a terrific social committee, also a very active bowls club – but you probably know all that. Do you play sport, Jim?"

"I used to like a game of tennis, but I find I don't really have the inclination anymore." Jim thought it best not to mention it was his heart scare that stopped him. "I reckon bowls could be more my thing, once we've settled in and got a routine established."

"Well, when you're ready, give me a call. I'll take you down for a roll-up. You can see if it's your type of thing." Robert stood up and made to leave. "I'll be seeing you at the resident's meeting tomorrow anyway, Jim. Oh, and if we, that is Harold or I, can help you to settle in any way, please give us a call." They both stood, shook hands and Robert made a quick exit.

Jim stood, looking after the man. He wondered if he had missed something. What was it about Robert that he could not quite identify; his charm, maybe his easy familiarity? *Hang on. He had said his partner, Harold.* Of course, they were the gay couple the gardener had mentioned to him. Jim decided to put his prejudice on hold, and reserve his judgement for the time being. He went back to the web page.

"What the hell?" The sound and sight of several people running past his office interrupted Jim's concentration. They headed out the front door towards the sound of raised, angry voices. Jim joined the throng gathered on the roadway in front of the building and pushed his way to the front. The raised voices had turned to high-pitched shouting. It took Jim a moment to appreciate the scene as he walked up to two women, who faced off near two vehicles in the middle of the driveway, one with its motor still running.

"I saw you do it on purpose. I'm lucky I had my wits about me and was able to move just in time to minimize the damage," said the older of the two.

The older woman's voice, still raised in rage, but no longer shouting, made Jim wonder how such a sound could come from such a tiny body. She walked around to the front of her car and examined the damage to her bumper.

"You were tailgating. You're just lucky there isn't more damage!" the younger woman yelled, just a few decibels lower than her older adversary. She walked over to Jim when he approached.

"Can I help here, ladies? Perhaps we should turn off the ignition first?"

Jim walked around the two cars. *Perhaps the one behind crashed into the one in front, or, maybe the one in front backed into the one behind*? he thought.

The women, voices now lowered to an almost normal level, each gave their version of events, and then several witnesses gave theirs. Who was in the wrong was apparent to Jim, but he was a diplomat and would have to choose his words carefully.

"I'm Elaine Steinberg from Unit 12, and I don't think you have to be a genius to figure out what has happened here," the younger woman said.

"Can you give your details to Mrs. ... ." He looked at the older woman.

She walked forward and held her hand out as she introduced herself to Jim. "Jessie Thornton."

"Jim Watersen," he responded. "Perhaps you could share details for insurance purposes?" Jim pulled a note pad from his pocket and handed it to Elaine, along with his pen.

The women walked to the side of the driveway behind Jim, and exchanged their information in an overtly civilised fashion, despite the fact that both were keeping a lid on their animosity.

Next, Jim cleared away the bystanders with some difficulty, and then looked again at the damage done to Jessie Thornton's car.

"It's not too bad. I'd be surprised if you needed to claim insurance."

They both nodded and Elaine looked at Jim.

"I'll not be paying for someone who maliciously ran into the back of my car. This woman has a vendetta going against me, and it's not the first time I have been accosted by her."

Jim was taken aback. He looked at Jessie for her response.

"No dog is safe in this place as long as Mrs Steinberg is at large. Two dogs have died from poisoning and all fingers are pointing at her." She pointed at the woman opposite.

"That is a serious accusation, Mrs. Thornton. I believe we have some issues to address." Jim was very careful to look at both women questioningly. "Why don't you park your cars and come into my office and we could perhaps sort this out."

They nodded and walked toward their vehicles.

As Elaine opened her door she said, within Jessie's hearing, "Bloody stupid, senile old bag." She slammed the car door and moved her car to the parking lot.

Jim tried not to smile. He had a feeling this was going to be an action-packed, fun-filled afternoon. The gardener popped his head up from the bushes growing around the entrance to the community centre.

"Better you than me, boss," he chuckled, as he lifted the grips on his wheelbarrow and made his way down the path.

During dinner that evening, Jim explained to Di how he had managed the situation. "It appears a couple of dogs have died in the last two weeks. The vet said they were poisoned, so now everyone is worried that it's someone from the village. Elaine Steinberg has complained about barking dogs on several occasions and has said that they should all be banned. Jessie thinks that Elaine should be banned, and they have both voiced their opinions publicly."

"Sounds serious. I do hope we don't have a dog poisoner in the resort."

"God, let's hope not. It's such a despicable act. I can never understand the mentality of people who do that. Anyway, it seems Jessie's dog was unwell today and she thought he was going to die. She was taking him to the vet, when she found herself driving behind Elaine, out of the front gate. She was so upset and angry; she simply couldn't resist shoving Elaine's car from behind. According to Jessie, Elaine was not moving fast enough."

"I swear, Jim, sometimes it's like living in the middle of a kindergarten."

"I know what you mean, love. The long and the short of it though, is that Jessie's dog, Ben, is fine this afternoon. Elaine said that she would like to be the person poisoning all the rabid dogs, but says it isn't her, and Jessie accepts her word on that. So, we still don't have a dog murderer, but we do have two very pissed-off old ladies."

Di raised her eyebrows and went on eating. A thoughtful frown creased her forehead, and she said, "Changing the subject for a minute, how much have you heard about the development on the other side of the lake?" she asked.

"Not much. I believe there will be about sixty new homes, all a little more salubrious than what we already have. Why do you ask?"

"I was at the hairdresser's salon the other day and I heard a couple of the ladies talking about the land there being unfit for development. They said there had been an old cattle dip on the site, and traces of arsenic and D.D.T. were found in the soil. They said it was great, because they prefer to keep the resort the size it is and they don't want to lose their walking path. Some of them are also very upset about losing their views."

"That's it!" Jim jumped up from his seat, almost upsetting his chair, "Poison – poisoned dogs!"

Di put both hands up to stop him going any further, and said, "Great minds think alike – that's what I was thinking. Do you think those dogs could pick up that poison from the grass over on the other side of the lake?"

"Well, of course. Makes sense, doesn't it? How can we find out for sure though?" said Jim.

"The Sleighmens are still here in Queensland, I believe. The area manager, Allen Sinclaire, said the other day that they would be here until council passed the development and the building commenced. So I wonder what they think about all this talk of contamination."

"They must know about it if we do, surely?" Jim said. "I'll ring Sinclaire tomorrow and see what I can find out."

******

"You're a hard man to catch," Jim said to the area manager, when he finally returned Jim's call.

"Places to go, things to do, you know how it is, man." Allen was always evasive, in Jim's experience, and Jim already had him marked as a sleaze. His business partner was Georgeina Bunning and it was obvious to Di and Jim that they were an item.

"I'm curious to find out if you've heard anything about the new development on the other side of the lake?" Jim asked Allen.

"Sure. It's all going ahead as planned, pretty soon, too, I believe."

"Have you heard anything about the land being contaminated?"

"Oh, that was just a vicious rumour, I hear they've done all the soil tests again and it's fine. Can't see why anyone would want to say something like that. It's in no one's interest to see that land lie useless. It's all going ahead, real soon. The boss says they're finalising the land sale contracts as soon as the council gives the nod – about a week, they reckon. What's your interest in it anyway?" Allen sounded suspicious.

"Oh, just curiosity – nothing else. There hasn't been any more trouble here since those protestors had their fifteen minutes of fame. I just like to keep on top of things. I hate to be the last to know and I can see this is going to be a great new project for us all."

"Yeah, yeah. Well, I've got to go." Allen rang off in his usual abrupt manner.

Jim was pleased not to drag out the conversation. He put the phone down and wondered what it would mean to the resort to have such a big extension; extra work for Jim and Di, perhaps?

Chapter Six

Council pre-election time was a busy period for everyone involved, despite the fact that most of the participants had been through the routine before, in some cases many times. Mayor Porterman was running for the top spot again but, with no one challenging him, he would be re-elected unopposed. He was delighted when he had found his expected opponent had withdrawn from the race before it had begun. There were a few new faces running for a position on council, including independents and a 'greenie bastard', as the mayor liked to describe the man to his inner-circle of faithful followers.

The 'greenie bastard', Laurie Lyall, had been scrupulous in his preparation. He had attended to all the legal requirements and had discussed his history with Peter, who was his campaign manager. They did not want any surprises to confront them at the last minute; certainly nothing negative that might sabotage his campaign at the crucial moment.

Marian was working flat out with all her usual commitments, plus attending functions with Laurie and doing letterbox drops in between time. "I have to say, I'm exhausted, but I love it as well," she said, and smiled at Laurie when he came in late after addressing members of the local Rotary Club.

He bent down to Marian, stretched out on the lounge.

She accepted his kiss with a loving familiarity.

"I just put a few more signs up on the way home. I hope these aren't taken down like the last lot – a bloody waste of money when they do that. Why can't people just play fair?" He flopped on to a chair and began to reflect on the night's events. "I'm pretty satisfied with how things went tonight, and how things are going generally. I'm finding Peter a wealth of information regarding my opponents; I had no idea he was so well informed. He knows so much about everyone. I'm glad he's on my team and I'm glad I'm not paying him - he's worth his weight in gold!"

"That's good, love; his wife is very nice too. We worked together yesterday and I found her quite dynamic, like her husband."

They sat together in silence, while the television flashed before them, each deep in thought and both too tired to get up and go to bed.

******

Mayor Porterman had also been busy that evening. A meeting with Roger Sleighmen had been unavoidable. The two men had only been in each other's presence twice previously; once in a crowd at a fund-raising for cancer research and the other at a university presentation. They had an intermediary, but Roger needed to discuss the rising costs of 'council co-operation', face to face.

They met in Roger's hotel room.

"Rising costs are making it impossible for me to do any more business here in South-East Queensland. I had plans for another resort development in your shire, but the expectations from your end have now made that prohibitive."

Colin Porterman paced around the room, hands clasped behind his back, looking at the floor. He could appreciate Sleighmen's concerns, but buying other people's silence was a costly commodity and, in today's climate of technology, difficult to achieve.

"I can't trust anyone," he said, "whether they approach me, or I them. It's too easy to leak information and still put your hand out for your cut. Loyalty is a thing of the past and everyone is a short-term operator; they're here today and gone tomorrow."

Roger put his hand up, both to acknowledge the mayor and to stop him talking. "I understand your position, but my pockets aren't that deep. The price now has risen out of my reach and, unless you're prepared to be reasonable, we can't do any more business."

Roger Sleighmen was adamant. As he later said to his son, he had no intention of paying the exorbitant 'donations' demanded by the coterie of council members who enjoyed the benefits of his largesse in return for favourable outcomes. Roger's philosophy was that there were other states with other councils; some with a members more than willing to play the game.

There was a long pause before Porterman spoke. "All right, leave it with me. I'll have to consult my colleagues. I'll get back to you."

They wound up the meeting with a perfunctory, grudging handshake and Porterman thought, *I'll see this bastard in hell before we do business again.* He noticed the expression on Roger's face and guessed that he may have much the same thought.

******

Andrew Sleighmen heard the door slam from his adjoining hotel room. He stepped out into the hallway and knocked on the door of his father's room.

"How'd it go, Dad?"

Roger shook his head, "Not at all. I'm finished with that bastard after this. He thinks he can pull my strings and I'll cough up any amount he demands. Well, we're not that desperate and he can go to hell. This current project is the last resort we'll do in this place."

Roger poured himself a whisky and threw it down his throat, like the angry man he was. He kicked his briefcase across the room and started swearing. "Bloody jumped-up dickhead – wouldn't know a good deal if it bit him on the bum!"

******

The resort development plan passed in council at the next meeting. There was some heated opposition to the development, but the numbers were not there to stop it.

Peter Dawson rang Laurie Lyall at work to give him the news. "Another win for the developers, mate. I can't believe how quickly this was pushed forward. Last I heard, they were investigating soil contamination. Now I hear all results were

50

clear and work starts as soon as the properties are vacated. Not only that, but it seems bloody obvious to me that the price of the land was first driven down and then snapped up by the Sleighmens as soon as everyone was ready to sell out."

"I agree it stinks," said Laurie. "Porterman is about as crooked as a country mile. His days are numbered though, mate. Just wait until I get in there and start breathing down his neck. I can't wait."

"That's my boy. That's what we want to hear, mate. We're going to get the bastards, big time. Hey, I'm looking forward to our meeting tonight. There's already enough money to start our campaign and we have no doubt about topping up the pot when we make a few calls, starting tomorrow." Laurie could hear the smile in Peter's voice.

All the members of CARP shared Laurie and Peter's enthusiasm. There were many other individuals as well, just waiting to see someone from the anti-development lobby get into council. There was a great deal of unfulfilled potential lurking just below the surface of Laurie Lyall, and he had a sense of the timing being perfect for him.

"See you tonight, mate."

"Too right," said Laurie.

******

Two sales agents employed by the Sleighmen Group were finalising the conditional contracts on the land adjoining the resort. There was an atmosphere of animosity when Sleighmen's men approached the landowners, and some of them tried to re-negotiate the deal. That was a forlorn hope; the Sleighmens were old hands at having watertight option conditions. The landowner's protestations were ignored, and the work on the property was set to start on schedule.

Andrew said, "This was actually easier than I expected, Dad. I didn't have a good feeling about this project when we began, but we'll have the earth moving equipment on site at the beginning of May. We can't ask for more than that now, can we?"

"We can always ask for more than that. Don't fool yourself; we have a long way to go yet. Think about the debt we've just incurred. The bank is going to want their first payment sooner than we get ours, so already we'll be dipping into funds that we've been keeping for a rainy day. That's why we pay our accountant more than he deserves."

Chapter Seven

Jim Watersen was a patient man. He dealt with all sorts of people every day. He thought nothing really surprised him and he had a rather cynical outlook on life. He was, however, unprepared for the events of that Sunday, his so-called 'day off'. He was heading around the back of the Clubhouse after enjoying thirty laps in the pool. It was a perfect summer day in paradise and Jim delighted in the knowledge that the luxurious pool and spa was there for his pleasure as well as for the residents. A pool service maintained it to perfection and he usually timed it so he had the pool to himself.

"Shit!" he shouted involuntarily, when he tripped on an obstacle as he came around a bend on the pathway. Jim stumbled and fell bum first on the ground. In front of him, under the low hanging fronds of a golden cane palm tree, he saw another person, crouching on the ground. He sat up and refocused on the man, who was hastily patting down dirt on to a mound under the palm.

"What the hell are you doing?" he asked.

"Sorry, mate, didn't mean to trip you. I'll get out of your way."

"Hang on, what are you doing?"

"I'm looking for Unit 26."

"What – in the dirt – under that tree? Give us a break."

"Oh, well, I just um … What's it to you anyway." The other man made to move away.

"I'm Jim Watersen, and I'm the resort manager, that's what it is to me. What were you doing, under that tree?"

The young man turned to walk away. "Fuck off and mind your own business," he said, as he looked down at Jim, still on the ground and wincing as he massaged his foot. Jim stood gingerly, but the man disappeared from sight by the time Jim took two faltering steps after him. Jim turned back to the palm tree and bent to examine the mound left behind. He scratched around for a moment and then felt his hand land on something hard. After a little more digging, Jim withdrew a metal box. Still kneeling, he opened the box and found nothing. It was empty. He knelt there, staring at the empty box for a moment. He was completely bewildered.

"What the hell?" he muttered to himself. He stood up with the box in his hand, and looked around the immediate area see if he had missed something. He kicked at the ground in a few different spots, found nothing, and then kicked the dirt roughly back in place.

When he arrived back home he found his wife dozing on the lounge. At first, he was reluctant to wake her, but she opened her eyes as he sneaked past.

"Have a nice swim?"

"The strangest thing just happened. I ran into someone who tripped me up. He was digging around a golden cane in the garden and then he swore at me and disappeared."

"Was he trying to take the tree?"

"No. He left behind an empty metal box, buried." Jim held up the box.

Di sat up and rubbed her eyes. "I need a drink. What time is it?"

"Funnily enough, it's drink o'clock and I could do with one as well." Jim made his way to the kitchen and a few moments later came back with a bottle of wine and two chilled glasses.

"Tell me again what happened. And why are you limping?" Di asked, as she accepted her glass.

Jim went over the story again and this time became more frustrated. "I should have gone after him; I may never know now what all this is about. Shit and damn." He sat back and went over the events in his mind again.

"Give us a look at the box." Di reached out and held the dirty thing away from her as she examined it more closely. "Must have had something in it – whoever it was has now taken the contents."

Jim nodded his agreement. "But what?"

"Hidden treasure?" She looked down at it again. "What did this guy look like?"

"Young, untidy, shaved head with a strip of hair left down the middle – tattoos on both arms, and neck."

"So pretty much like every other young person hereabouts, nowadays?" Di said disgustedly.

"What about drugs?" Jim wondered, almost to himself.

"A mighty strange place to keep drugs, don't you think?"

Jim did think – all evening and half the night. He planned to go back the next morning and examine the site again – and start asking questions as well.

Because he was a highly organised person, Jim was usually ahead of his work and had time to talk to people. That next morning, at the front door to the Clubhouse, he met Matthew Weatherlee, the resort salesperson.

"I've been meaning to catch up with you, Matthew, but I've been so busy ... ."

Matthew interrupted, "It's okay but, here I am now and it's nice to meet you, Jim. I believe your wife is with you."

Jim nodded.

"I have my sales office in one of the unsold houses, so I move around a bit; depends on what's vacant at the time."

"Of course," said Jim "We need to get together; I hear I will be replacing you on your days off."

"That's the usual plan, but it depends how you're going. There have been a few little problems here lately. We don't want to stress you out to the point where you decide it's all too hard."

"Well, we're tough. Di and I hope things will get back on track, real soon. It's my hope that we can co-operate and work harmoniously."

"Don't see why not."

"Good, good. I have a situation that you may be able to help me with. It involves a young man, whom I don't know, but maybe you can enlighten me about him."

Jim went on to tell Matthew about his meeting with the young man on the path the previous day.

Matthew listened, nodding from time to time. "Well you're right, I don't know who this person was, but please, give me a day or two and I may be able to come up with some answers for you. I suspect he may be someone I know, but let me check it out first, please."

Jim agreed. He watched Matthew Weatherlee stroll off to his office.

******

Allen Sinclaire finished his mobile phone conversation as Georgeina Bunning walked up and opened the car door.

"Who was that?" she asked, when he was free.

"Head office. We've got to check on the furniture being imported for the display units. Let's go down to the wharf now and see if it's offloaded yet." Allen put the car into gear, and squealed the wheels as he took off, as usual. On the way out, they passed two men standing outside their house, looking at their garden. It was No. 39, the home of Harold Smith and Robert Wieland.

"That's that pair of poofs," commented Georgeina, "It's hard to believe a couple of men that age could still be entertaining one another. I mean, what's the point?"

"Don't ask me, love. I think they should both be shot. A disgrace to the male population, I say."

Georgeina cuddled closer to her lover, "Not like us love, you could certainly be proud of yourself." She giggled and nuzzled Allen's neck.

"Best decision I ever made – taking you on as my assistant."

"I'm not your assistant. You know I'm your equal partner," she said, as she drew back, indignantly.

"Well, we both know all about that equal opportunity shit. You're learning though, aren't you? Don't worry, I'll teach you everything I know."

Georgeina's attitude became instantly frosty. "How little you know about this industry. I can assure you, I'll still be in this job long after they've pissed you off."

A wry smile spread across Allen's face, as he mused that she knew less than nothing about his extra-curricular business activity. That was something he would not be teaching her.

The pair of bigots drove on in silence.

Chapter Eight

E   *lection day. The day of reckoning. The day my life could change. What am I doing, for God's sake?* Laurie Lyall's thoughts had gone round, and round, and round all night ... and into the morning.

There's a stillness in the air, just before it rains. You realise you've been waiting for it when it finally happens, Laurie thought, as he lay in his bed, suddenly aware of the quiet patter of rain on the roof. He looked at the red numerals on the digital clock for about the tenth time that long night and morning. *Four-o-seven. Damn, if I haven't slept up until now, I might as well give up*. He eased quietly out of the bed and started for the shower.

"Is it time to get up?" Marian squeaked.

"No, no, go back to sleep. You come down after eight, as we agreed. There's nothing you can do until then."

Marian rolled over and was quietly snoring almost immediately.

Laurie slipped out of the house at 4.30am and drove down the deserted streets to campaign headquarters, where he found Peter and the rest of the group just arriving. They all soon had a cup of coffee in their hands and were going over final plans for the day. There was excitement in the little office and a sense of camaraderie that translated into belief of success.

"So, who are you sending to cover division two?" Laurie asked Peter, as the campaign manager walked around, handing out lists to all assembled.

"Jonathan. He's our youngest."

Jonathan smiled at the mention of his name. He was looking so proud to be able to contribute to what he hoped would be the start of Laurie's political career. The polling booths set up in that division at the local primary schools had a large population of first-time voters and middle-class greenies. Jonathan would be able to talk to the voters when they arrived, charm them with his broad smile and enthusiasm. Even if he was preaching to the converted, he obviously loved every minute of it. Peter had flagged him as a future politician himself; he would be one to watch.

After an hour of animated discussion, the group broke up. They gradually dispersed to their cars, in pairs, to take up their positions at the many polling booths across the Shire of Westbridge.

Laurie looked at Marian. He loved the way she had her silky hair tied up in a big clip on top of her head. It set off her round face to perfection, her glowing complexion and quick smile as attractive to Laurie as the first time he had seen her. He had never loved her more than he did that day. He knew what it had cost her to throw away her inhibitions and support him through all the uncertainty and long days. This would be the longest of them all.

The rain stopped and the sun began to shine. The first voters started to trickle in to the booths.

******

"Congratulations! You've done it, boy. The best man won, and it's you," Peter said. "Good news, great news, just wait until that bloody Colin Porterman walks into the chamber and has to look at your shining face. His days are numbered!"

"Oh well, I wouldn't go that far, but I'm sure as hell going to give him a run for his money in a few years. See if I don't."

They lined up to pump Laurie's hand and smack him on the back. His face was beginning to hurt from the permanent smile that was pulling his mouth apart.

Laurie Lyall was now a full-time councillor. He would be resigning from his job in computer repairs and taking on the problems of the shire. He, as much as anyone, was aware of the responsibility that he was taking on and he was serious about making a difference. Government corruption at any level was abhorrent to him and he truly believed humankind was innately good; or, perhaps at least leaning that way. He smiled to himself when he thought of several councillors who would not be happy to see him sitting next to them. He really was ready for this next step in his life.

******

The Maxwell Excavation Company had won the contract to do the clearing and preparing of the land for the Sleighmen Group.

"I expect to have the whole three hectares ready for the earthworks to commence in two to three days," said Adrian Deemarko, the engineer in charge of field operations for Maxwell. Charlie Gibbs, his chief plant operator, nodded. They stood with maps spread out on the bonnet of the truck and surveyed the area to be commenced.

"I hope to get all this surface stuff cleared by tomorrow and then Gene can come in with his heavy machinery the following day," said Charlie.

The boss nodded, rolled up his maps, and strode back to his vehicle. He left Charlie to get on with what he was best at.

At 7am sharp, the first bulldozer turned over its engine. It shattered the silence and the roar set dogs barking and caused birds to take to the air. The work of clearing the land on the far side of the lake had begun. The morning was cool and crisp, and bode well for a good day's work.

It was just before lunchtime the following day when Charlie halted his dozer abruptly, and jumped down from the cabin. He left the engine running as he strode around to the pile of rubble in front of his dozer.

"What the ... ?"

He walked right up to the clods of earth and tree branches piled up in front of him. His eyes widened and he craned his neck in amazement as he peered at a jumble of bones. They looked like human bones. He bent down, gingerly touched one, picked it up, and turned it over several times. He reached out and gathered several more, which he examined carefully.

"I'm no fuckin' forensic scientist, but these sure as shit look human to me," he mumbled to himself. He laid them down carefully and walked back to the dozer where he pulled himself up to the cabin, turned off the engine and picked up his mobile phone. His hand froze.

Think, Charlie, think. What could this mean? Charlie sat still for several minutes, contemplating the ramifications of his find. *This is probably an old cemetery; in which case it must be unmarked, because even very old cemeteries are usually recorded somewhere and noted by local councils.* Charlie had not seen any head stones or old cement mouldings. *What if they are aboriginal bones?*

Charlie was one-eighth aboriginal. It would be hard to identify his heritage just by looking at him, and it suited him that way. He had had a good education and was paying off a nice home where he supported a wife and three daughters. He was only rarely involved with what he called 'aboriginal affairs'.

"But this could be a sacred site," he said loudly, to reinforce the importance of the find to himself. He knew what he had to do. He also knew that if he told his boss, there was a good chance the find would disappear. The Sleighmens, he knew, would not be above ploughing the bones back into the earth. If the find meant a delay to the project, then it would be in their interest to bury it, literally.

Charlie rang his mate Mick at work. Mick worked in the local council as a ganger on the roads. Charlie remembered that Mick had once told him they had discovered bones, later found to be aboriginal, when they were excavating an area for a park.

"I'm glad I caught you, mate. Got a minute?"

"Sure, bro."

"I have a problem and not sure what to do about it."

"And you're askin' me? That's a joke. We're on smoko, so make it quick; you know I don't like to miss anything."

"Yeah, sure. Okay, well I think I've just uncovered a pile of aboriginal bones. Like a sacred site or something."

"Shit! Bloody hell. Who have you told?"

"No one yet. That's why I'm ringing you. I've worked for this mob before and they would have no ethical concerns about getting rid of the lot."

"Can't do that, mate."

"I know."

"Can you sit on this for a while? I need to contact a bloke from the Aboriginal Land Council. He will know what to do. I'll have to get back to ya."

"Sure." Charlie hung up. He got down and fossicked around for some soft tree branches. He covered over the find, climbed back into the dozer, and backed his machine away from the site. He spun the giant machine and moved to another area to continue work.

As Charlie gouged and pushed the earth, his mind slipped back to the time a few years previously. He was among the land-clearing group that prepared the site for the original resort, on the other side of the lake. Sleighmen's marketing promoted it as a lifestyle resort. The concept was becoming more and more popular with the Over 50s, many of whom wanted to retire in a gated, secure, and well-appointed facility with a community of similarly minded people. Charlie had no doubt that Roger Sleighmen was a shrewd businessman, who could see that the ageing population of baby boomers would provide a source of income for years to come. Charlie had always acknowledged Sleighmen's business acumen and had been impressed with how

Sleighmen pressed all the right buttons with his product. With resorts scattered around Australia, Sleighmen ensured each establishment reflected a suite of facilities tailored to the local physical and economic environment. Charlie gave him credit for reading the market and supplying a first-class product to satisfy the needs of his demographic target, but Charlie also had reason to think that the Sleighmens were a bunch of crooks. Based on what he heard about how they had acquired the land in the first place, and how they treated their employees and contractors, he had no reason to want to do them any favours – like giving them advance knowledge of anything like an aboriginal claim on this land. He smiled at the thought of fat old Roger Sleighmen paying out money for land he couldn't develop, or, at the very least, couldn't develop without a protracted and expensive foray into the pedantic world of due, legalistic process. He laughed aloud as he thought, *Maybe it's time to get some of your own medicine back, Mr. crooked-as-a-dog's-hind-leg Sleighmen.*

It was much later that day when Mick finally rang Charlie back. "Sorry to take so long, mate, but I had trouble finding the bloke I wanted. He's on his way over to ya now. You'll see him in a Toyota Cruiser with four other blokes. They all know what they're about, so just take ya lead from them. Okay?"

"Yep, thanks Mick. Actually, I think I see their vehicle over near the gate now. Catch you later." Charlie cut his engine and walked toward the four-wheel drive, making its way across the partially cleared land toward him.

The vehicle stopped in front of Charlie. He could make out Adrian Deemarko's face behind the wheel. The front doors swung open, emptying Deemarko and a man Charlie recognized as Andrew Sleighmen, onto the freshly scraped dirt. Two executive types with highly polished shoes slid to the ground from the back seat, their shoes immediately swallowed by the soft earth. The shine disappeared under a layer of fine dust.

Deemarko said, "What's been holding you up, Charlie? I thought you'd be done with this by now, you know what a tight schedule we have."

Charlie castigated himself for not realising there was more than one Toyota LandCruiser in the world. He had to think fast. "That area over there can wait until I've cleared these trees; we have someone coming to drag these out first. I'll get to that tomorrow." Charlie turned toward the area he was working on and tried to re-direct everyone's attention away from where the bones lay under the branches.

The afternoon sun was setting as the men gathered around. Andrew Sleighmen pointed as he said, "That strip there, where the internal roads meet, will continue to another security gate. That flat block of ground is set aside for a park, a barbecue, and recreation facility for families. About half the new homes will front the lake and will have a private walkway passing through a group of specially selected native trees and shrubs, indigenous to this area. These prestigious, three-bedroom, two bathroom homes will all have a view from a large deck looking out to the bushland in that direction." He pointed toward the mountains in the distance. "Personally, I can't think of a better spot for my retirement than this great climate and such a fabulous setting. I believe this type of facility will soon generate demand that exceeds supply; not that there is much around to compare with what we have planned here. I'm not aware of anything else in

South East Queensland to come close to this. There are resorts on the Gold Coast and in other states, but the latter don't have our climate and all are much more expensive than what we are offering. This is the best-value-for-money Over 50's resort we have ever built, and we are the professionals in this market." Andrew turned and smiled at the two bankers. He had them in the palm of his hand. They looked around quietly and allowed the information to sink in before they started asking questions.

Charlie was getting worried as he watched the men wander over the property, and he deliberately placed himself between them and the bones. Several times, he redirected one that was heading toward the bones mound by pointing out the beauty of the native bushland, and the small wildlife that still lived on the perimeter.

"At sunset you'll see wallabies grazing in that grassy paddock over there," he said as he pointed, "and the bird life, it's amazing, especially in the mornings."

"Won't that all change when the development starts?" said the younger looking suit, standing next to him now, and taking a genuine interest in what Charlie was talking about.

"Not the way we work. We pay great attention to the effects our works will have on the environment, and we're especially keen to minimise the impact on the local wildlife. We're sensitive to the effects of noise and habitat disturbance and have an environmental group monitoring our progress." Charlie regurgitated the spiel he had been told to direct toward such visitors as those in front of him today. He knew it was crap, but he liked the sound of it and knew he was within the hearing of the developer. He looked up as he heard the approach of another vehicle.

A Toyota LandCruiser drove up to the bulldozer and four Aboriginal men stepped down. Charlie walked toward them, extending his hand and introducing himself.

Andrew Sleighmen's group looked on curiously and Andrew walked up to find out who they all were.

"So, boys, what can we do for you?" asked Andrew. He was full of confidence and, as the owner of the property, looked a little put out by the appearance of a group of uninvited people on his development.

The aboriginal men introduced themselves. One of them said, "We're here at the request of the local Aboriginal Land Council. We have reason to believe there may be sites of interest to us, sites we have previously been unaware of."

"What are you talking about?" Andrew was getting edgy.

"We've been notified by an interested party that there may be human remains in an indigenous site in this area, a site that has been previously overlooked."

"What?"

Charlie stepped forward and pointed to the pile of branches. "It's over here, fellas."

He took the lead and they all walked over to the mound of tree branches. Charlie reached down and removed the covering, exposing the pile of bones. There was more than one gasp of astonishment.

For a moment, no one spoke, and then the Land Council men began to examine the bones more closely. They nodded, mumbled to each other, and walked around picking up and putting down separate bones.

Finally, the one who appeared to be in charge said, "We'll have to examine this site more closely; in the meantime the whole area will be closed down. There is no question in my mind that the area needs a thorough investigation. A court order will be forthcoming. The police, and of course the Coroner, will be contacted right now."

Deemarko, Sleighmen, and the bankers stood open-mouthed, listening to the declaration by this stranger. The sun began to descend on the tableau. No one seemed to know what to do next. It was Charlie, who finally asked, "What precautions do we need to take to protect this site, right now?"

There was a hushed conference as the aboriginal men considered what they should do next. The senior man said, "We'll stay here until we can arrange around-the-clock supervision of the area. We can't risk any interference with the site and all work on the site must cease immediately."

Andrew shouted, "No! You can't do that. We have a schedule to meet and I won't tolerate interruptions to the flow of work. I don't care what bones are buried there; we have commitments to honour. If you wish to remove your bones, fine – but we will not stop work."

"We will have a court order in the morning, sir."

"Look, I don't give a damn about a bunch of prehistoric bones. This is my property, and you are trespassing – the lot of you. You can take your friggin' bones and all clear off, right now!"

The older of the indigenous men spoke up. "I'm sorry, sir, but what we will do right now is leave three men here. I suggest you get in touch with your lawyer and clarify your own position, sir." He walked back to the vehicle and returned with a roll of orange plastic barrier. He and his friends began to look for rough poles to knock into the ground so they could form a temporary fence around the area.

Andrew Sleighmen was already on his mobile phone. The rest of the men wandered around talking quietly to one another, while Adrian Deemarko cornered Charlie.

"What the hell do you think you're playing at, Charlie? Why wasn't I the first one you consulted? Have you any idea what this could mean to our contract? This company pays our wages, and bringing in outsiders to a situation like this pretty much tells me where your loyalty lies."

Charlie looked directly at Deemarko. He allowed him to finish, and then said, "You know, we both have a responsibility to protect sacred sites. When I started with Maxwells, I was subject to the same orientation process you were. We can't ignore the fact that this could be an important find and must be treated that way."

"Why the fuck didn't you call me first?" Deemarko shouted into the face of the larger man. "I'm the one who has to answer to the boss. You'll be wearing this mess, mate. I mean it. If anyone is hung out to dry, it won't be me."

Deemarko turned, and almost tripped on a clod as he departed angrily.

Charlie watched him go and knew it was the truth. He could lose his job over this. He should not, of course, but Charlie knew these bastards would find a way to dismiss him that would look legitimate, and appear to have nothing to do with this incident. One thing was for sure, he realised there would be no reference to take to the next employer. He walked over to where the indigenous men were organising themselves for a long night.

Andrew came back through the murk of the early evening, blundering over the rough ground in his haste. He stopped a couple of paces short of the men, waved a pointed index finger at them and almost spat as he said, "You pricks are going to be hearing from my lawyer in the morning, so don't get too bloody comfortable."

"Bastards," he said, as he turned and waved his arms around, herding his guests to his 4WD.

******

"We've arranged to get a camp site set up here," said the older indigenous man, "There'll be a ute along soon with tents and supplies, so we'll take it from here, Charlie. Thanks for sticking your neck out. I know this might have consequences for you and I hope you don't lose your job."

"Yeah, me too. What happens now, mate?"

"We go through a process. We'll have specialists out here and we've got lawyers working for us. It won't take long to verify whether this is a one of our burial sites, and we should be able to tell the origins of the bones and identify how old they might be. I know a few noses'll be out of joint, but that's tough. We've lost more than one sacred site in this area, thanks to the likes of Roger Sleighmen and others. They couldn't give a bugger about us and our culture, but they're quick enough to go around slapping preservation orders on things their culture values, and they haven't been here more than a couple of hundred years. Geez, I recently read about a 1950s house that's had an order put on it – because of its significant cultural value. Hell, Charlie, my people have been here for forty-thousand years!" He shook his head and turned to talk to one of the other men.

Charlie decided it was time he left. He had done his bit and now it was time he went home and told his wife he probably would not have a job for much longer. The stars began to stand out in the night sky as he drove through the gate of the construction site. He wondered if he would be back again.

Chapter Nine

Jim had not heard from Matthew Weatherlee regarding the mysterious metal box. He saw him frequently, even waved from a distance, and was aware of his going in and out on resort business, or so he presumed. As the weeks slipped by, Jim realised he had allowed the daily chores of running the resort to push the box episode to the back of his mind. He resolved to pursue the matter with more vigour and found the perfect opportunity late one afternoon, when he saw Matthew farewelling a couple from the sales office.

"Matt? Can you call in at the office on your way home tonight, please?"

"Sure, Jim, no problem. See you in five."

Matthew closed his mobile phone, tidied some papers on his desk, and locked his office door behind him. He drove his white, soft-top SAAB the short distance to the parking area in front of the community centre. He looked back at it as he walked away. He loved that car; it represented how he saw himself and his future. As he knocked and entered Jim's office, he switched his thinking to the issue at hand. He knew what that was going to be.

"Nice to see you again, Jim. Sorry I haven't been back to you about that issue of the buried box, but there's no light I can shed on it. I made some enquiries, but without success, I'm afraid. I've still got feelers out, but I doubt there will be anything forthcoming." He sat down on the chair Jim pointed to.

"Well, that's disappointing. I was hoping no news was good news, but can't be helped, I guess. How're sales going?"

"Not bad. You should have my last week's report on your desk by now."

"Yes, of course – I meant, off the record."

"It's all the same. I think some people are waiting now for the new development, not rushing to buy something that may look second best as soon as they open up the luxury villas. Actually, the way they're selling off-plan, I don't think there will be any to put on the open market."

"That's good, I'd say. I'm looking forward to seeing them. I saw a lot of people over there today; first the construction equipment, then this arvo, more vehicles. It looks like it's steaming ahead."

They walked together to the car park.

"Look, I can see lights over there, still. Who could that be at this time of night?" Jim asked.

"Let's take a look," said Matthew. They strode out together to the path that surrounded the lake. A few minutes later, they came upon the little gathering, setting up tents by torchlight.

"What the hell do you think you're doing?" Matthew shouted, as soon as they saw people setting up camp.

An old Aboriginal man came forward, waving his torch. "And who are you, mate?" he asked.

"Not your mate, that's for sure. We're employees of the owners of this land. This is private property. You can't camp here."

"We've already notified the owners. Andrew Sleighmen was here earlier. He's aware we're protecting a possible sacred indigenous burial site. Tomorrow there'll be investigators out here, and in the meantime, all work is on hold."

Jim and Matthew were dumbfounded. They could not think of a thing to say. Finally, Jim asked the man, "Who else has been informed, like, do the media know about this yet?"

"Not so far as I know, sir; certainly not from us, anyhow."

"Okay, thanks," said Jim, and the two men walked away, both deep in thought about what this would mean to the company.

"Can you imagine what this will mean to a development that has to run strictly on schedule?" Matthew said. "It's a developer's greatest nightmare, uncovering an aboriginal site, and watching your investment go down the drain. Shit, I wonder what'll happen."

"Not our problem, really, is it?" Jim knew it would have little to do with his day-to-day job.

They arrived back at the parking lot. "Let me know if you have any thoughts about that other business, will you?" Jim said, in parting.

"Sure." Matthew was already directing his thoughts elsewhere.

He thought about Jim's assailant and thought he knew who it was. *Probably Kevin,* he thought. *He's the only bastard around here stupid enough to bury drugs where he had to dig them up in public. Still, no one would ever have thought to look in the garden, under a tree. Just bad luck Jim came along at the wrong moment.* Matthew knew about his ex-mate, Kevin, and how he made a good living selling drugs. Kevin was also a gardener, and he was planning to apply for the assistant gardener job at Keeala Resort. Matthew wondered if Jim would recognise him when he applied, or if Kevin would now look elsewhere. *This place is such a good cover, that's the trouble, Allen found that out and so did I. Allen has already picked up the furniture from the wharf and no one suspects the hidden drugs. Now Kevin wants in here. No wonder he already had drugs planted around the place.*

When Matthew arrived home that evening, he was completely engrossed in his own thoughts. He sat down to his dinner and said barely a word to his mother. She loved him so much, it did not matter. She was always happy to see her golden child.

Chapter Ten

When he arrived back at the hotel on the following evening, Andrew went to Roger's room and found him shouting into his telephone. Andrew had never seen his father so angry. After a couple of minutes, Roger slammed the receiver down in mid-statement, which suggested to Andrew that the other party had hung up in his father's ear. Andrew gave him a wide berth and slipped into his own room, closing the door quietly behind him. A moment later, it flew open.

"You idiot! I can't rely on you do anything properly. What's the use of having a dog if I have to do all the barking myself?"

"Oh, so I'm your bloody dog now, am I?" Andrew said, as he swung around to face his father. The man stood in the doorway. His bulk filled it from jamb to jamb.

"Nah, on second thoughts, that'd be an insult to a dog. A dog's intelligent enough to be trained, but you, you useless prick, well, what good are you? You're supposed to be the project manager but we end up with the whole bloody shebang on hold. How the hell did those bastards get wind of a so-bloody-well-called sacred site, on our property?"

Andrew clenched his fists, took a deep breath, and counted to ten before he replied, "The excavator operator – he was the one who called in the Aboriginal Land Council. He's probably one himself. He saw the bones and contacted them, and they came straight out. They in turn, contacted the police. There was nothing we could do. I'm planning to ring that solicitor who represented us in that injured employee compensation case. You remember him?"

"Yeah, I do, but I'll bloody speak to him. I want to make sure we get on to this straight away, without any more cock-ups," Roger said, as he moved his portly frame into the room.

Andrew sighed as he tried to keep control of his anger. He said, "Please yourself, but I suggest you get a little more under control, though. If you want his help, there's not much sense putting him offside as well, is there?" Andrew walked past his father before he had a chance to respond.

"Where's his friggin' number, anyway?"

"Why don't you try looking in the phone book – it's right in front of you – careful it doesn't bite you. Anyway, he won't be there now, will he? Some people keep office hours, you know. I'm going down to dinner."

"Fuckin' smart arse," said Roger, to his son's disappearing back.

******

The following morning, Roger left at 8.30 to see Stephen Brigges, the solicitor. He had taken his briefcase stuffed with papers pertaining to the development. He felt positive, and was sure they would have work rolling again by the afternoon. In his experience, money greased most wheels and spoke all languages. Brigges arrived just as Roger got out of his cab. They walked together to his office.

"How can I help you, Roger?" said Brigges, as he motioned him to a seat.

Roger squeezed his large frame in one of the office chairs and began rummaging through his briefcase.

"Like some coffee?" Brigges tried again.

Roger shook his head, and grunted, "I want to get down to work." He dumped a pile of papers on the solicitor's desk. "We need to get to the bottom of this today. I can't afford any bloody hold ups."

Brigges picked up his phone and told his secretary to cancel his appointments that morning. He turned to Roger. "I have certain commitments later in the day that can't be postponed, so let's see what you have."

He pulled the mess of papers toward him and considered how much he should indulge this rude, arrogant man. Previous dealings had left him not wanting to continue with the relationship, but he knew that, unlike some of his other clients, Sleighmen's money was good, very good. Brigges also grudgingly acknowledged that, much as he disliked the man, he always knew exactly where he stood with Roger Sleighmen.

Roger looked up under his brows at Brigges. "Money talks and bullshit walks. Don't forget it. I didn't get to where I am today by pandering to every Tom, Dick and Harry."

Brigges acknowledged the other man with a nod. "Tell me what's been happening," he said.

******

Andrew sat in front of his computer, a freshly brewed coffee steaming on his office desk. The company bank statements spread out before him. He stared. He knew there had to be an explanation for the figures he was looking at. *There's something wrong here, something seriously wrong.* He pulled out the latest report from the Chief Financial Officer, Randell Thompsen, dated a week previously. Andrew had not spoken to him since then. He picked up the phone and connected with the secretary in his office in Adelaide, South Australia.

"Hello, Sue, it's Andy. How's the weather there today?"

"Not as good as Queensland, I'll bet, Mr. Sleighmen. How can I help you?"

"Let me speak with Randell Thompsen, please. I presume he's in the office?"

"As a matter of fact, no, he's not. I haven't seen him for a couple of days. I thought he was off sick, but I haven't had an official confirmation of that."

Andrew thought for a moment. "Connect me with the General Manager then, please."

"Simpkin speaking."

"Hi, Neale, it's Andy. I'm trying to catch up with Randell Thompsen but not having any luck ... any idea where he might be?"

"No, haven't seen him, Andy. As a matter of fact, all I've had is an email from him a few days ago, saying he's sick and he'll probably be off for a couple of days. I have a long-standing appointment with him in about an hour and I've just this minute been trying his mobile to check whether he's coming. There was no answer; just got the *Phone switched off or out of range* message. Tried his home phone as well. No luck there, either."

"That's a bit strange. He can't just absent himself like that. Someone should know where he is. Can you search him out and get back to me straight away? The shit's hit the fan here and we've got the project on hold. Yesterday, they found old bones on the work site and now the locals are claiming the bones are from some sacred bloody site. Can you believe that?"

"That's not good, Andy, not good at all. I've had experience of indigenous sites and the negotiations can drag on forever. What are you doing about it?"

"Dad's at the solicitor's office right now, trying to get a court order to overturn the suspension order."

"Well, good luck with that – and I'll get Randell to ring you as soon as I contact him."

Andrew paused for a few seconds before he said, "Nah, listen, on second thoughts, don't tell him I'm looking for him. When you make contact, just let me know where he is, pronto, okay? Oh, and tell Sue that if she speaks to Randell, she's not to mention that I was asking for him. Comprende?"

"Sure, but what's the problem?"

"I'm hoping there isn't one, Neale. Look, I can't go into details now, so I'll be in touch soon. Oh, and do us a favour will you, and don't let on to Dad that Randell's not in. Thanks, mate."

Andy rang off before Simpkin could prolong the conversation. He did not like to keep him uninformed, but thought discretion was called for in case there was a simple explanation for what was before him on the desk. The sinking feeling in his guts betrayed that hope.

* * * * * *

Georgeina Bunning did not hold a grudge – in fact, she was an easygoing person. She enjoyed Allen Sinclaire's company. The sex was great, different to that she shared with her husband, Maurice – completely different. He was so considerate, while Allen took what he wanted and expected Georgeina to do the same. He liked it rough and he had brought out a side of her that she had not known existed. She blinked to clear the sleep from her eyes and looked at her lover as he slept, stretched out next to her.

He's getting old - grey stubble sprouting from his chin, he has a pot belly, Georgeina thought, as she lifted his arm thrown comfortably across her chest. She stepped lightly to the bathroom, hoping to have another hour or so before they both had to rush off to work.

Fancy calling me his assistant, Georgeina thought as she looked in the mirror. *What an arsehole. He has no idea what I know about him from his file. He's hanging in there on a wing and a prayer, that's all. He'll be lucky to have another year in this job. Then I'll choose my assistant/partner.* She laughed to herself as she thought about seeing Allen's report in the staff file. He was not popular with management, and she now had more influence than he did. *Next year, he'll be out and I'll be able to decide where I'll work. Andrew Sleighmen has made noises before and I know what he likes.*

Allen shouted, "You there, girl?"

He threw the sheet back and stumbled to the bathroom, in time to catch Georgeina getting out of the shower. He turned her round and guided her back through the glass door. She began to giggle and he started to grunt. This was what they both called a good start for the day.

82

******

Midday approached. Andrew had not heard from Neale Simpkin. Eventually, fed up with waiting, he called the office again.

"So where is he, Neale?" Andrew got straight to the point.

"I wish I knew. I'm getting worried; someone should know where he is. I've rung his home phone and his mobile several times since we spoke. No answer. I'm just now thinking of sending someone round there. Maybe he's had a heart attack or something."

"Yeah, maybe, but look, go all out on this, will you? Drop anything that's not urgent and get me some answers. I'm getting a really bad feeling about this. Call me soon." Andrew rang off and scratched his head. He couldn't do a thing until he spoke to Thompsen, and he was getting agitated with the lack of progress. He had not heard from his father either, and he knew that would be a complicated, and probably acrimonious discussion, when it took place.

The phone rang. It was the bank manager. He wanted to see Andrew.

'No, we need to discuss this in person, Mr. Sleighmen, as soon as possible."

Andrew put the phone down. *Oh, shit. This is all I need.* He wished he had spoken to Thompsen first, as the CFO had all the latest figures relating to the loan for the Keeala Resort development. He headed straight down.

The manager's personal assistant ushered Andrew into the manager's office. The bank's loans officer sat to one side of the manager, behind a huge wooden desk. Computer printouts covered the desktop.

"We have a problem with the figures from your head office, Mr. Sleighmen," said the manager.

"What sort of problem?"

"The account is empty."

"What? What do you mean, *it's empty?*" Andrew asked. He felt faint, and tried to control the panic that suddenly churned his insides. He dreaded what was coming.

"I mean there's nothing in the account from which we usually draw your loan repayments. It has been systematically emptying for months. We presumed you knew what you were doing – that you were simply moving money around. That, of course, is your business – it's your money – but now we're waiting for a repayment and there is simply nothing left to draw from. Well, I shouldn't say there is nothing left – there's a balance of $100.00."

Andrew continued to stare at the men sitting opposite him. His mouth fell open. "What do you mean, systematically emptying? We don't access that account at all. As you know, it was set up specifically to service the last loan."

"Have you spoken to your accountant, Mr. Sleighmen?"

Andrew tilted his head back and looked at the ceiling. He said quietly, "No, we can't find him."

He lowered his gaze and made eye contact with the bankers. Some sort of mutual understanding dawned on them. For a moment, there was silence, then Andrew turned and stood up. He started walking around the office, looking at the carpet and wondering if it was a good quality and why anyone would choose such a bland colour. Then the light in his brain turned on again. He looked back at the men behind the desk and shook his head.

"I can't give you any explanation right now, but I suspect you're thinking what I'm thinking. I'll speak to my office and ring you back later today. I pray to God there's a reasonable explanation for all this confusion."

They parted, and Andrew was on his mobile phone before he got into a cab. By the time he reached the hotel, he was no wiser about the money or the accountant. He was not looking forward to telling his father – as if there were not enough problems already.

Chapter Eleven

"**O**ut of order. Out – of – order!" Mayor Colin Porterman shouted above the din to make himself heard.

He was tired and it had been a long day. The noise in the chamber was deafening and he felt like walking out. A woman at the end of the room had the floor, but was not able to speak loudly enough, despite having commenced her opening sentence at least three times. Several councillors were deliberately drowning her out with their interjections, even though she had not had the opportunity to say her piece. Finally, the hubbub quietened enough for her to be heard, and she began to speak in support of a proposal made by new councillor, Laurie Lyall. He had made quite a lengthy speech about the parlous state of the sewerage plant, his submission supported by references to information contained in highly regarded consultant's reports.

"Effluent is known to be leaking into the nearby creek," continued the female councillor. "Evidence was presented last year to show that the creek was polluted with many bacteria, including E Coli. As stated by Councillor Lyall, there are dead fish on the lower reaches of the creek and tests show conclusively that they were killed by the pollution from the sewage works. The repairs to the plant have previously been deferred, due to either lack of funds or apathy on behalf of the elected council. It is simply not good enough to defer this any longer. I propose that the plan submitted by Councillor Lyall be accepted and be handed to the Chief Engineer as soon as possible. This matter must be treated as urgent. We all have families that could be affected, especially if we have further flooding." The councillor finally completed her speech and sat down amidst overtones of grumbling and objection.

The debate continued for another twenty minutes before the vote took place. The motion carried and the chamber erupted. The mayor was red in the face.

When the meeting concluded, Laurie approached his fellow councillor Rose, and thanked her for her support. "Getting something like this up, amid so much opposition, is quite a coup. I'm delighted to have you onside and look forward to working with you again," he said.

"Thank you, Laurie. I believe we agree about many social and environmental issues. To think that some others would rather see our resources spent on fireworks and a balloon display at the end of the Westbridge Show; it makes you wonder how some of our councillors determine their civic priorities. It's not just public health issues like the run-down sewerage infrastructure, but there are so many really essential projects crying out for attention, I can't, for the life of me, fathom where their brains are, although, on reflection, maybe I can. Being ladylike, I'd better not say where, eh?"

"Their brains are focused on popularity and getting re-elected. The Mayor thinks froth and bubbles can buy the constituents' votes, but he underestimates their intelligence – as he will find out when he goes to the polls." Laurie smiled conspiratorially.

This was a great beginning for Laurie, and he was quick to place a call to Peter to let him know the outcome of the voting. He said, "I'm gratified to see I have support where I wasn't expecting it. If we continue this way, I may someday say I'm proud to be a councillor serving in a council with an honourable mayor in place."

"Someone like you, maybe," Peter laughed.

******

For the developers of the Keeala Resort expansion project, things were not going so well. Roger Sleighmen arrived back at the hotel around three in the afternoon. He was sitting, staring out the window, when his son knocked on the door.

"Enter!"

Andrew opened the door and walked to a chair, where he sat without speaking. He waited for Roger to acknowledge him.

Roger did not turn to look at his son, but rubbed his face in a washing motion as if to bring himself back to the real world. After taking a few laboured breaths, and without rising from it, Roger twisted his chair so that he faced Andrew. He steepled his hands in front of his face; a face that conveyed nothing but contempt.

He said, "I've got some disturbing news, and I'll need your full attention. I have the impression you aren't particularly interested in the outcome of my day with the solicitor." Roger breathed deeply; he looked as though he was trying to control a rage that was quietly boiling. His head trembled as he looked at his son, as if wondering why he bothered with him at all.

"Of course I want to know how things are going. This is my company too – you're not the only person working here." Andrew stood, took a step, and then hesitated.

He was about to walk up to Roger, but thought better of going anywhere near his father. The temptation to hit him was greater than he had ever felt before.

He sat down again, clenched his fists, and ground his teeth for a few seconds. He took a deep breath and said, "So, what did happen today? What about the court order to stop work?"

"It still stands. We see a magistrate tomorrow, but according to the useless, fucking solicitor, there may be nothing we can do to push things any faster. We're at the mercy of archaeologists and forensic scientists and the Land Council. The place is considered a crime scene until proved otherwise. The presence of human remains gives the Coroner control over the whole area."

"So, the project is stalled. Well, you may think that's either a bad thing or a good thing after you hear about my day. Randell Thompsen is missing."

The rise and fall of the big man's chest increased and was the only movement in the room. There was not a sound anywhere except for Roger's wheezing. Roger closed his eyes. When he opened them, he made eye contact with Andrew.

"What the fuck do you mean, *Randell Thompsen is missing*?"

"He's gone! No one knows where. He emailed Neale a few days ago and said he was ill, and may not be in for a couple of days. We've been trying to contact him all day. I've just spoken to Neale and he's had people looking in all the usual places, like his unit, his family, his club. No one has seen him. Neale's reported him missing to the police."

"I don't bloody believe this. Ah, shit, what about the bank? Have you looked at the accounts?"

"They're empty."

"What do you mean, *they're empty*! It's not possible. Have you been down to the bank?"

"They rang me. I was with the loans officer and the manager this morning, then went back to see the manager this afternoon. Our personal accounts haven't been touched, but the three accounts on which Randell had authority to operate are virtually zero. The bank's security section is on to it and conducting checks into the transactions over the last twelve months. You know I keep a weekly check on all the accounts. I have no idea how he was able to remove funds without attracting my attention."

Andrew stopped and put his head in his hands. He sighed, sounded almost as if he would cry, but then looked up again and said, "We could be bankrupt by tomorrow if we don't find that bastard immediately."

"So," said Roger, "the bank's waiting on a loan repayment, but what about all our equity, our long standing relationship with those blood suckers? We're totally dependent on this new project to get us back on top. They know we're on a winner. We've sold most of the homes off plan – they'll just have to wait and see us through this." Roger seemed to have become unnaturally calm.

Andrew said, "Sure, but, as of today, we have no money and no project. We're completely frozen."

"*Frozen*? That's one word bloody word for it. I can think of another word starting with 'f' that would describe our situation more accurately.'"

Roger walked to the window and stared. He stood there for a couple of minutes, his shoulders heaving, then pivoted his bulk to face Andrew.

"Jesus H Christ, Andrew, how could you bloody well let this happen?"

Andrew's shoulders drooped as he looked down at his lap, as if to close out the world. He looked up again and saw his father watching him tremble, his legs first, then his hands. Andrew knew he was going to cry but managed to stand and walk to the bathroom. He could feel Rogers eyes following him, and he knew his father too, would be in a state of turmoil he had not known for many a year.

Chapter Twelve

Bad news travels fast and, on this occasion, one may have thought that good news did too. The stop work order on the land clearing by the lake was hot gossip the day after the injunction had been issued.

"From what I hear, most of the residents will be happy to see that land left undisturbed. What's the company's reaction?" Harold asked Jim, while he watched the manager tidy up the notice board.

"It's all a bit of a surprise, I'll say that. I don't have any idea how the company will handle the situation. There are people over there today – investigators, and I hear they have very tight security. We'll have to wait and see. We'll probably be the last to know."

"I haven't seen anything of the new gardener," Harold continued, as much asking a question as making a statement. He looked at Jim, expecting an answer.

"What new gardener?"

"Before you arrived, there were plans afoot to employ another gardener. The old one, Tom, had about as much as he could handle and there was advertising out for another. Maybe it got forgotten in the handover."

"There was no handover; we had to pick up the pieces as best we could. Allen Sinclaire and Georgeina What's-'Er-Name are always busy doing something, but don't get me started on that."

"So does this mean we won't be getting a new gardener?"

"Not at all. I agree we need another badly. Do you know if anyone applied for the job?"

"No, but I think Matthew, the salesman may know of a few relief people we've had here from time to time."

"I see. Well, Harold, you've given me my project for the day. I'm off to check the files and I'll talk to Tom. Thanks for bringing it to my attention."

"It's okay," Harold laughed, "it is my absolute pleasure."

He waved and was gone. Jim picked up the phone in his office and called Matthew. The salesman had a few suggestions and said he would send them around in the next few days.

Good, thought Jim, *What's next?*

******

"Interesting news about the find over on the other side of the lake, don't you think, Jim?"

"What's that?"

Jim turned to see a resident with his hand out.

"Richard White, from number twenty-six. I see they've found an old cemetery over on the new development. Hard to imagine they didn't know about it before."

Jim nodded slowly, wondering how much he should say. "Yeah, hard to imagine," was his non-committal reply.

"They say it's from the early settlers. I guess that's an end to the proposed development."

Jim knew this bloke was fishing. "It's all very interesting, isn't it?" Jim turned back to his desk and smiled. "We'll probably be the last to know."

The other man could see he was not getting any news here, so he said, "I'll see you later then, Jim."

"Sure."

Jim waved, and shook his head, thinking the man was not only fishing for information but he had the facts wrong to start with. Jim thought about a conversation he had had with Robert Wieland and how they concluded that the resort and similar groups were a microcosm of society. 'We have one of every type, shape and size. Good, evil, bullies, victims, leaders, followers, and someone always gets the story wrong, but it doesn't stop them from repeating it,' Jim had said.

Two days later, Jim interviewed three prospective gardeners. The last one was Kevin. He seemed to know his business and came recommended by Matthew.

"When can you start, Kevin?" Jim asked.

******

"So who did you employ?" asked Di, later that evening.

"Guy named Kevin; sounds keen and is qualified. Well enough presented, tidy hair cut and so on. I had the feeling I'd seen him somewhere before, but couldn't place where. Whatever, he starts tomorrow."

******

"I think you better come and take a look at this." The onsite archaeologist was laying out long bones on a sheet he had spread on the ground next to his dig. The two men bent over the bones and together began to put them in the outline of a human body.

"So, these are nothing like the others, are they?"

"No. These are quite recent. All the others are very old – indigenous skeletons, I'd venture. I'm going to put in a call to the coroner. I think this may turn out to be a crime scene." The man pulled his mobile phone out and dialled.

The two men guarded the scene until the police van arrived.

******

The local police called in excavator operator, Charlie Gibbs, for an interview. After some discussion, they all went to the area where he had discovered the bones. Charlie was amazed at the change in the whole site; some areas had been pegged out, and markers were dotted here and there.

Rick, the indigenous leader, approached him when he arrived. "Good to see you, mate," he said.

They shook hands and walked together to where Rick was guiding him. Charlie was aware of the two police officers hovering in the background and wondered why they were there.

"Now, can you point out where you were when you first discovered the bones?" This came from a man in white-overalls, scrabbling through a pile of soil. He looked up as they approached, and stood and wiped dirt off his hands.

Rick whispered, "He's the archaeologist."

Charlie nodded, and began to get his bearings as he walked around the site. "I was about there." He pointed close by, then crouched down, and looked at the ground as though taking a level. "Yes, I must have uncovered them with the first sweep. I was lucky to have noticed them at all. The morning sun hit something shiny and I just happened to stop before I swept them away."

"So how deep down did you go?"

"Not deep at all, they were just below the surface, all piled up, if you know what I mean."

"Yeah, sure. Can you describe how you found them – I mean how they were lying?"

"They were in a pile, like I said, all shovelled up together. At first, I just looked, but when I picked one up, I knew it was a bone. I was pretty confused at first, but then thought this must be an old cemetery. But that didn't make sense either, because if it was a cemetery there would have been cement covers and headstones, like. Now that I think about it, I think they looked as if they had been dumped there, all together. Do you know what I mean?"

"I do. Yes. Well, is that all you can tell me?" the archaeologist hesitated, then, as Charlie nodded, he walked away.

Charlie felt disappointed he could not help more. He turned to see Rick talking to the police.

They broke off their conversation with Rick and a barrel-chested sergeant approached Charlie and said, "There are a few things about this case that don't quite fit. I believe you were on the crew that cleared the land on the other side of the lake – for the original resort?"

Charlie nodded and said, "That's right, couple of years ago."

"And nothing unusual occurred at that time?"

"Nothing – well, except the protests of course, and you're likely to get those no matter where you clear land. The

'Greenies' are out in force, no matter what you do. They found koalas in the trees on the other side – tried to stop the development going ahead – didn't want the habitat destroyed, you know?"

"But the project did go ahead, I see?"

"Of course. The koalas just disappeared, and the protesters gave up and went off to stir up some other developers. We're the silly buggers in the middle – greenies on one side, and developers on the other. We get the blame, no matter who wins. But we're just doing a job; got to earn a living."

"Yeah, I understand your position. So, you don't know what happened to the koalas?"

Charlie laughed. "Well, let's say I have my suspicions. They had to disappear, didn't they? You can't hold up a major development for the sake of a few cuddly koalas. Mind you, they made an unexpected appearance there in the first place. Before the notice of the development went up, no one could remember ever having seen any there before. So who's playing games here? On the one hand, the greenies plant a koala, and on the other, the developer makes it disappear. It's all just a game, isn't't?"

"Are you working again now, Mr. Gibbs?"

"Got some casual work. Don't know how long that will last and I won't be getting a reference from Maxwells, that's for sure. Like I said, you're dammed if you do and you're dammed if you don't. Might have to go and work in the mines if I don't get something soon."

"Let us know if you're planning to move away then, will you?"

Charlie nodded his agreement and they drove him back to his car in town.

As he drove home, Charlie wondered what it was all about. What was so strange about his find? He knew it could be very significant, if they were aboriginal bones, and he also knew the developers, the Sleighmens, would be really put out. But why the police? What had they to do with all this?

Later the next day, everyone was packing up at the site. All the bones had been removed, and many sink holes and small digs had been filled in. It had become clear to the investigators that the bones had been planted there, and not all that long ago.

******

Roger Sleighmen flew back to Adelaide. As he pushed open the main door to the Sleighmen Group offices, he started to shout, "Don't any of you lazy buggers know where Randell Thompsen is?"

A stunned silence from the staff greeted him. He pushed a sliding glass door off its tracks as he stormed through to the passageway that led to the office of his general manager. There was no pretence of manners or respect, as he barged into Neale Simpkin's office without knocking.

"For fuck's sake, Neale, how long does it take to find one skinny bloody accountant, eh? Why did no one tell me that Randell was missing? Didn't it seem odd? Suspicious? The fact that no one knew where he was should have set off some bloody alarm bells."

Roger slammed his fist down on Neale's desk in frustration, and accompanied that with a string of expletives. Coffee spilt from a mug on the desk. Roger's face reddened and breath struggled to escape his heaving lungs. He slumped in the chair facing the desk.

Neale Simpkin mopped the spilt liquid with a tissue. He said nothing. He waited.

Roger fished in his shirt pocket, pulled out a half sheet of small, white tablets and mimed at Neale for a glass of water.

When Neale returned with the water, Roger tossed two tablets into his mouth, snatched the glass from him, and gulped the contents. There was no 'Thank you', only a long, guttural belch across the desk.

There was a period of silence again before Roger shouted, "Well? What have you got to say for yourself? Eh?"

Neale did not answer immediately. He waited for his anger to subside enough for him to reply in a relatively calm voice, "I don't keep tabs on everyone, especially executives. Randell's always answered directly to you, or Andrew. He's also never kept regular hours, come and gone at will; we had no reason to be suspicious. His weekly reports went directly to you and Andrew. We only met at the monthly meeting or as required, or we talked on the phone."

Roger was already looking away. "Did you contact that private investigator I asked about?"

"I did, but he was reluctant when he heard we had no money. He'll be in here this afternoon, nevertheless, to meet with you."

"Who fuckin' told him we had no money?"

"He didn't have to be a genius to work out that if he's looking for an accountant who's emptied our accounts, then it'll be a pretty fair chance we'll be left insolvent."

Neale could see the sweat bead on Roger's head and run down his neck. He wondered how high Roger's blood pressure was and how he would react to what he was about to say.

"I'm afraid I have more bad news and this is something I want you to know now, rather than later." They stared at each other.

"Well, don't stuff around, for Christ's sake. Out with it."

"I've been offered another position. I'm giving you notice that I'll be leaving at the end of the month – that's if you want me to stay until then. Otherwise, I'm happy to leave now."

"So someone just walked in here and thought you looked like you could do with a job. Pig's fuckin' arse!"

Neale said nothing.

Roger could see Neale was struggling and he was not going to make it any easier for him. He guessed he must have been looking for another position since he heard the news of the company's financial situation. Roger stood and clenched his fists.

Neale took a step back, as though to suggest Roger was going to strike him.

"You snake, Neale. Think you're deserting a sinking ship? Well surprise, surprise, we're not sinking, you bastard. How can you leave after all we've been through together?"

"That's just the point, Roger. We have been through a great deal together, but I've had enough. You're an arsehole of a man with no concern for the feelings of others. I've made excuses for you for years. I've defended you in the face of so much criticism, including of the way you treated employees who were shown the door just when they needed your support. So it's time you felt what it's like to be left out on a limb. Like I said, and it's against my better judgment, I'm prepared to give you until the end of the month. I'd walk right now, but that would be bringing myself down to your level of ruthless behaviour. It's up to you, Roger. You know where to find me."

Neale walked past Roger and slammed the door behind him.

Dumbstruck, Roger stared at the closed door

******

"So, how much experience do you have with this sort of crime?" was Roger's first question.

The other man opened his mouth to answer but Roger cut him short.

"What do you know about my situation?" Roger had a no-nonsense inflection to his question.

The investigator started to answer, but Roger overrode him again. "I expect you to be free to start immediately, or you needn't bother."

The other man leaned back, crossed his arms, and gave an exasperated sigh. He waited for Roger to finish his list of demands. When Roger stopped to draw breath, the man spread his arms wide, palms upward, and raised his eyebrows as if to say, "Finished?"

They sat silently, and looked at one another for several seconds. The investigator threw a manila folder on the desk between them. "My credentials, and, to answer your question, I know nothing about your situation except that your accountant has apparently put a big hole in your moneybox. What I do know, is I can't start until the day after tomorrow."

"This dickhead could be in South fuckin' America by then!"

The investigator ignored the jibe and said, "I want $5,000 upfront before I begin, and, just so there's no misunderstanding later, you can see my daily fees and out of pocket allowance in front of you. My bank details are all there. Take it or leave it." He sat back and clasped his hands behind his head.

Roger looked at the 'Schedule of Fees' in front of him and opened his mouth to protest.

It was the other man's turn to dominate the exchange. He put his hand up and said, "I'm not the one facing ruin here. Listen, I don't work for nothing. I'm not cheap, but I get results. I can guarantee you'll get your money's worth, but if you want to try to save money by going to some cut-rate outfit, be my guest."

Roger shut his mouth and looked out the window as his fingers tapped on the desk. "Right, let's get on with it," he said.

******

Muriel Jacobs had a good head for finance. She was confident of her abilities and she decided it was time her boss knew it. They met in Roger's office and she immediately opened her laptop and brought up some figures.

"These are Randell's latest figures. As you can see, he began to get a bit sloppy of late and he didn't try to hide his transfers over the last couple of weeks. I don't understand that, but I suspect a good IT expert will be able to tell us where he was when those transactions were made."

Roger leaned away from his assistant and looked at her. "So, you're telling me *you* came up with all this information yourself?"

Muriel reminded herself that *misogynist* was a word commonly used to describe her boss, but she let the slight pass and said, "I've taken a look at our overall situation. After Andrew and I discuss a couple of details, I think I can come up with a few suggestions to help us keep our head above water, until we catch up with Mr. Thompsen. I'm sure we can chase him down, via the money trail. He was, as you probably know, an inveterate gambler."

"No, I didn't know that. How did *you* know? Is it common knowledge?"

"Not at all, but he let a few things slip in conversation once or twice. One doesn't have to be a gambler to recognise one. Only last year, he lost his family and his home because of his financial difficulties."

"How come I hadn't heard all this?"

"Maybe you just weren't listening. The other executives were aware, I believe."

Roger stared at his assistant. He could see she knew what she was talking about.

Muriel knew Roger had always undervalued her and others. She knew there would be no risk of self-recrimination on Roger's part, for the way in which he had just spoken so dismissively to her. He was so insensitive and crass, Muriel had often thought, that he would not even realise his behaviour was so unacceptable. Muriel could not help thinking about how often she had overheard Roger belittling his son, accusing him of incompetence and neglect. Rarely had she ever heard him acknowledge Andrew's achievements. She wondered why Andrew had stuck it out so long and hoped the day would not be far away when she would only have to deal with him. For now, she had enough self-confidence to work without the recognition and respect she deserved. Her day would come.

Chapter Thirteen

The coroner looked at the forensic report. Frustrated, he re-read it, and threw it down on his desk. Because of the suspicious nature of the body's discovery, he resolved to hand the investigation over to the police, but doubted he would see any results soon.

A shadow appeared on the frosted glass panel of the coroner's office door. There was a quick knock.

"Can I come in, Martin?"

"Ah, Frank, good of you to come so soon. Take a seat."

Detective Frank Pekalski walked into the office, seeming to take-up a lot of space with his large frame. He sat and smiled at Martin.

There was an easy familiarity between the two, which had evolved over many years. While neither would claim best friend status, they both shared a cordial respect for each other's values and professional capabilities.

Frank asked, "What have you got for me, mate? I've a clear calendar today, so I'm at your service."

"Just as well you're not pushed for time. This is going to take longer than a day though, but you're welcome to get started." Martin slid the report across his desk. "Another case to take up our time. There were some relatively fresh human bones dug up with some very old aboriginal bones."

"Yeah, I'm aware of it."

"Problem is," said Martin, "it doesn't fit any of our investigations over the past couple of years. How come no one knows who's bones these might be?"

Pekalski sighed several times as he read the report. Satisfied he had not missed anything important, he closed the file, placed it on the coroner's desk and said, "So, not a clue then?"

The other man shook his head and said, "Not a bloody thing. It's up to you to dig up something, so we can put this case to rest; even if it's a 'done by person or persons unknown' result."

Pekalski stood and thrust his hands into his pockets. His brow furrowed as he paced first one way, and then the other. Finally, he picked the report up again and put it under his arm. "Well, won't get it done pacing around here, will I? I'll be seeing you then, Martin."

They gave one another a casual salute and Pekalski closed the door behind him.

When he returned to his office, Frank Pekalski already had a few ideas about where he would begin. The usual processes would have to be gone through, just to dot the i's and cross the t's. Frank knew he would have the drudgery of going through missing persons reports, assault records where victims had used false names, suspicious hospital admissions and so on. Not really expecting any of these usual lines of enquiry to yield any helpful information, Pekalski decided to be more pro-active and pay a visit to Maxwell Excavations.

Start at the beginning and then let the story unfold for itself, he thought. He sat in front of his computer for the next two hours. When he came up for air it was almost lunch time, so he left the comfort of his air-conditioned office and picked up a burger on the way out to Maxwell's office. The manager there was of little help but Pekalski did leave with the address of Charlie Gibbs.

******

Pekalski was thorough and perceptive; he had a good imagination but kept grounded with a firm grasp on reality. All this meant that he could often guess at probable outcomes, based on his keen awareness of human nature and a little psychology. When he had looked at the file in the coroner's office, a particular name cropped up more than once, and in different contexts. Pekalski's interest had been aroused more by intuition, rather than what he had read in the report. He decided to visit Laurie Lyall at the council chambers.

Frank met Laurie Lyall at the entrance to the council offices, as had been arranged. He introduced himself to Laurie and got straight down to the reason for the interview. As they began to walk towards a courtyard, Frank said, "I'm investigating the discovery of skeletal remains on the site of the Keeala Resort expansion. I believe you're familiar with the site and that you were around when the previous development was commenced? By that, I mean the first stage of the resort on the eastern side of the lake?"

"I was, and it stirred up quite a reaction at the time. There was strong opposition, that's for sure. I know you'll probably think I'm biased, but I genuinely believed there were rock-solid grounds for rejecting the application for the original project. That land had significant wetlands and a huge bio-diversity factor. It had always been known as a wildlife habitat, even though it had been used as a bit of a dumping ground as well. They should have cleaned it up and then put a protection order on it. It could have been used as a nature park and bikeway. Even a picnic area and playground would have been better than covering it with buildings. The project obviously gained approval. There was a lot of talk after that about corruption and abuse of process within the council. Now, we have the same story doing the rounds about the expansion of the resort."

Frank and Laurie were walking around the outside of the council chambers as they talked. Frank pointed to a bench. As they both sat down in the shade of a Morton Bay Fig, Frank said, "I get from your response that you're pretty passionate about the environment generally."

"Well, yeah. It's very important to me and the main reason I ran for local council. I want to be around to see changes in the way our community cares for the area, but part of caring for our environment is having checks and balances on the people who administer the laws and regulations that affect that stewardship. I'm sure internal corruption is nothing new to you, Detective."

Frank had a wry smile as he shook his head in acknowledgement.

Laurie smiled conspiratorially and said, "I've seen too much of it, close hand, and I don't like it. Without naming names, there are individuals in positions of power who may be going to get their comeuppance, with a bit of luck."

"When you talk of corruption, I have the feeling you know people willing to go to great lengths to get what they want," Frank said.

"I guess calling it, *going to great lengths,* is one way of putting it."

"In a way, we're after the same thing. But I think you have more freedom than I and you're not constrained by rules in the same way the police are."

"True." Laurie had to listen closely now, as much for what Frank may not be saying as what he was.

"The case I'm working on at the moment involves a homicide a couple of years ago. You're no doubt aware of the indigenous burial site uncovered at the Keeala Resort expansion site recently."

"Yes, but I only know what's in the news, basically. I heard they've stopped work and it may not be restarted if it proves to be an ancient burial ground. I know, also, that the Aboriginal Land Council may choose to remove the bones and bury them somewhere close by – somewhere safe. Despite some ill-informed members of the community thinking otherwise, they're generally a pretty reasonable lot and they're usually prepared to sit down and negotiate sensibly. Human nature being what it is though, you can't blame them for playing hard-ball if they come up against someone who tries to crash his way through negotiations. I know from previous experience, that the developer, Roger Sleighmen, is one of those types. He doesn't like losing and won't give up easily. I've had dealings with him and he's not an easy man to get along with. He's arrogant and greedy and he'll fight to continue that development – no matter who he has to walk over. We've all heard stories about his heavy handed tactics, of course – hell, I suspect he was behind a drive-by shooting at my place. Trouble is, like a lot of these guys who live on the fringes of the law, they distance themselves effectively from the actual offence and you can't convict on rumour and anecdotal evidence."

There was a long pause while Frank thought how best to get the information he was looking for. He said, "I heard about your shooting. I wasn't on that case, but I remember there was a bit of talk about it in the department at the time."

"Yeah, it kept the public entertained for a couple of days. What happened was, early one morning a car drove by and peppered our house with shotgun pellets and rifle bullets. Your guys don't know who did it and they weren't even able to locate the vehicle used. It was a bit unsettling really, to be a target and not actually find out what the message was or who was leaving it. Still, as some of my mates said to me, you wouldn't have to be too bright to come up with a name," said Laurie. "No reflection on you guys, of course," he added quickly. "Like I say, suspicion is one thing, proving it is something else altogether."

"Well, you're absolutely right about that, Laurie. I've actually had a quick look at the file on the case. There's been some speculation of course, based purely on educated guesses; like you've done, I suppose. Unfortunately, there's no proof. So far, there's nothing based on fact that we can go any further with. What's your best guess at who it may have been?" Frank looked directly at Laurie as he asked the question.

"For all the good it'll do me, I believe it was someone hired by the developers of the resort to scare off us protestors. I was the leader of a group called CARP – Campaign Against the Rape of the Planet, at the time. I'd headed a protest at Sleighmen's city office a couple of weeks prior to the shooting. You know, the thought has occurred to me that maybe Sleighmen thinks CARP planted those bones to put a stop to this latest work. CARP didn't. I mean, where the hell would we get bones from? Even though I'm no longer a member of the organisation, I can guarantee they had nothing to do with interfering at the new site."

"I see. Well, you're a brave man, Laurie Lyall, but aren't you concerned you may still be in the firing line, even though you've officially disassociated yourself from CARP? Are all the people in CARP as determined as you?"

"Well, most are very committed and prepared to give it their all. They've all come up against opposition, some of it pretty ugly and personal, and even from within their own family members. But, that's the price, isn't it – of having ideals, I mean."

"Has anyone ever been injured in the course of a protest?"

"Of course, there was my incident. Luckily, we weren't hurt, except for a cut on my leg, but yes, a few others have sometimes been assaulted physically at protests, sometimes psychologically. I mean, they've been quite affected by the resistance."

"How do you mean?"

"One example would be my old friend, Jon Chamberlaine. He just disappeared and was never heard from again."

The detective swung around and looked at the side of Laurie's face. He was suddenly alert. "What? Tell me more about this Jon Chamberlaine. Please."

"Jon was a leader in the fight to have the original Keeala Resort development stopped. He worked very hard and had a lot of support, but I believe it could have been the strain of maintaining the fight that drove him to leave. It's my belief he probably couldn't handle the pressure and the threats and just took off. He didn't tell any of us, just suddenly dropped out of sight. No one's heard from him since."

"What about family, friends?"

"A far as I know, he didn't have any – family that is. He never spoke about anyone. He lived alone in a tiny cabin on an acreage property, not far from the CARP headquarters. He owned practically nothing. The owner supplied the furniture and stuff. I went out there once, in fact, it was only a few days before he disappeared. As I say, he had little in the way of personal possessions, just his clothes, and a few personal items, but he did have some photographic gear – he was a talented photographer – and he had an old Jeep. He used to garage his Jeep in a shed at the CARP place and he kept his camera gear in the vehicle. That was normal because he lived within walking distance, and the shed was secure. His Jeep was up on blocks. I think he was waiting for some spare parts to arrive. At the time he disappeared though, we all thought it a bit strange that he'd left his cameras behind. We figured he must've wanted to travel really light and disappear. There'd been several attempts to intimidate him so, as I said, I – we – thought he'd cracked under the pressure."

"So, what sort of intimidation was he subjected to? Like what?"

"Well, threats in the mail, abusive emails and phone calls, that sort of stuff, and his dog was left on his doorstep with its head bashed in. That happened not long before he left."

Frank nodded and took his time before he asked the next question, "What makes you so sure he went voluntarily?"

"Well, I guess I'm not 100% sure. At the time, we reported his disappearance to the police, but because his personal stuff was gone from his cabin and there was no evidence of foul play, he became a forgotten man, just another missing person. What puts some doubt in my mind though is the fact that he's never contacted anyone. Look, I can understand he may have been seriously scared off, but a couple of us were really good mates of his. He would have known, beyond a shadow of a doubt, that he could've relied on our discretion if he'd contacted us. That's what really puzzles me, the lack of contact."

"It sounds like his disappearance is a matter I should follow up."

"But why now? It's been a couple of years, and like I said, they never found any evidence of foul play."

"Laurie, what I'm about to say is off the record. I believe you can be trusted to keep it confidential?" Frank raised his eyebrows to Laurie.

"Absolutely."

"We found what we suspect are Caucasian bones in the ground at the excavation site, last week. We know they're not anything like as old as the indigenous bones. It appears they were dropped in together to hide them."

"So, is what you're saying, those bones may be Jon's? Is that what you think?"

Pekalski was silent for some time before he said, "I'm not saying that at this stage. It's only now that I've heard about Jon Chamberlaine from you that I think it warrants further investigation."

They both stood and began walking back to the entrance to the council chambers. They shook hands on parting and Pekalski said, "I'll be in touch as soon as I have anything. In the meantime, don't hesitate to let me know if you think of anything of interest in regard to Mr. Chamberlaine, anything, no matter how trivial you may think it is."

"I will."

The councillor walked up the steps, a million thoughts going through his head, mostly about Jon Chamberlaine. With a jolt, he thought, *What if Jon was killed? What could that mean for me?*

Chapter Fourteen

"I don't know how you did it, mate. You must be a bloody good actor," said Matthew Weatherlee.

He stood in a grassed area at the rear of his display unit. He had heard a mower and had gone to see if it was his mate, Kevin. Kevin smiled smugly at Matthew's remark. He knew he could put on a good performance when required.

"Mate, you're not the only one around here who can be charming when necessary. I remember you thought you had all the girls under your spell at school – until I came along, that is. Remember what happened then?" Kevin said.

He smiled as he pushed the big ride-on mower into the gardener's shed. He had been working as second gardener at Keeala Resort for two weeks and the management had no complaints; not yet.

Kevin found it easy to ingratiate himself with his affable, easy-going persona, but his disarming public manner hid a darker side. He was easily bored and he found a release from the tedium of day-to-day living by pushing drugs. The interactions with his clients and suppliers and the constant need to be vigilant about police activity, gave him adrenaline rushes that overcame his boredom.

He made a good living moving drugs around and used them himself occasionally. He knew he would lose everything if he got hooked, but sometimes could not resist a hit; got him through some very difficult times. He knew he did not want to end up like some of the druggies he supplied.

His biggest challenges came from his competition. Unless he kept his supply accessible, demand could disappear at any time and between his pick-up and later distribution to his clientele, his stock was always at risk, even from desperate clients who could not pay and for whom stealing was their only alternative. He also had to keep his sparse records secure; they too were valuable.

"If you're going to hide stuff around the place, mate, don't tell me about it," said Matthew. "I'm not getting caught up in any of your illegal schemes. Remember, I've got myself and my mother to support and I don't need you messing it up."

******

Matthew sounded very righteous but he had his own deal happening. He called it his 'nice little earner' and was surprised when Allen Sinclaire had somehow discovered his scam. Sinclaire had confronted him and threatened to expose him unless he got a piece of the action.

"I know how it works, mate," said Sinclaire. "You don't refurbish the resales, you just give them a quick once over and put them back on the market – charge the owners big bucks for non-existent carpet replacement and repairs and pocket the profits – a nice little earner. Well listen, mate, from now on, I'll have half, thank you very much. Don't try to gyp me either, because I've been in every type of scam you could think up. You're just an amateur, boy; don't ever cross me or you'll be very, very sorry." Allen was so smug and confident. Matthew wished he had never started the scam. Now, he was stuck with it.

******

Allen Sinclaire did not share any of the information about Matthew Weatherlee's rip-off with Georgeina, nor did he ever hint to her at the source or extent of his own very lucrative income. He collected drugs hidden in furniture that came from Indonesia to the wharves in Brisbane. He passed them on to a contact and answered to his real boss in Brisbane, Jack Noonan.

Noonan was the joint-head of one of the biggest drug syndicates in Australia, together with his brother, Norman, one of Queensland's best-known politicians. Jointly, they made a formidable team and had successfully amassed a fortune; most of it discreetly laundered and buried deep in a morass of shelf companies and secret bank accounts overseas. The brothers rarely met in public, their competition grudgingly respected them and did not interfere with their mutual businesses. It was an old family enterprise and, although known to the police, they were rarely engaged with them. Their arms reached way up the chain of political influence, and they had access to some very sensitive and confidential information. To further their interests, they had threatened on more than one occasion to use it.

Allen Sinclaire's front was as area manager for the Sleighmen Group and it gave him the opportunity to move around the country easily. One way or another, he was a very busy man.

******

Frank Pekalski knew he was on a trail, he could smell it and he picked up the pace. His next visit was to the office of CARP. Laurie Lyall had suggested he talk to a Peter Dawson. 'He'll be the most likely to be able to tell you something about Jon Chamberlaine.', he had said.

"How can I help you, Detective?"

Pekalski sat on a dilapidated cane chair opposite Peter Dawson, also on a cane chair, but one in a slightly better state of repair.

They were meeting at the CARP headquarters, a small timber house in a bay side suburb, close to the waters of Moreton Bay. An elderly founder of the organisation had donated the property to CARP, along with a nice piece of wooded acreage.

The two men sat in an old bedroom, converted to an office. Pekalski soaked in the atmosphere and became aware of a feeling, different from any other place of business he had ever been. First, there was the smell, earthy and soft. There was the aroma of coffee and freshly baked cake in the air. Voices and laughter came from the kitchen. The windows were all open to the sea breeze, which was cool and refreshing. No one seemed to be in hurry, and both men and women moved from one office to another. There was a large notice board, dripping with information. Frank could hear music, some kind of ethnic string instrument, and he wondered if it could be Ravi Shankar; he smiled when he thought he was the only Asian musician he knew.

Pekalski turned to the reason for his visit. "Peter, I believe you had a member here by the name of Jon Chamberlaine."

Peter nodded, almost imperceptibly, as if reluctant to say anything.

"Laurie Lyall said you may be able to shed some light on his disappearance."

"I don't know why he would say that; he knows as much as I."

This time, the detective nodded, and pushed on with his questions. "What can you tell me about him? How long was he involved here before his disappearance? Has anyone heard from him since?" Pekalski asked.

"I'm glad you are referring to him as having disappeared; no one else at the police station seemed to take it too seriously, at the time."

"So, you believe he did not just move away of his own volition?"

"Well, look, we can't be sure, but he didn't seem the type of person who would leave all his friends and his job without some notice."

"He was a photographer, wasn't he?"

"Yes, and very successful at his art, I must say."

Peter pointed to the wall behind Frank.

Pekalski turned and saw a series of beautifully framed wildlife studies. He stood and examined them more closely.

Peter said, "He was a sensitive and exacting artist. He took his involvement here very seriously and we are the poorer for the loss of him."

Frank resumed his seat and listened as Peter warmed to the subject of a man for whom he obviously had a great deal of respect. Finally, he looked directly at the detective and asked, "Why are you only now investigating Jon's disappearance? I mean, has there been some word of him?" His look was suddenly expectant.

"We're investigating the identity of a skeleton, found in an excavation site, near Keeala Resort."

Peter sucked in a breath and stared into the detective's eyes. "Oh, God. I don't know what to say. Do you think it may be Jon?"

"I believe the possibility is worth checking. I don't suppose you have anything here that was his personal property? We would benefit greatly by being able to do a DNA analysis."

There was a slight pause, before Peter said, "Oh, stupid me. It's been so long it had gone out of my head. Yeah, we've got Jon's Jeep in a shed down the back. When he came here, he was planning to get rid of it, but then he decided the organisation might find it useful because it was a 4WD. We did use it quite a bit at first, whenever Jon wasn't needing it, but it was out of action when he disappeared."

They walked together to the back of the house. "Has it been used since his disappearance?" Frank asked.

"No. It's up on blocks. We'd loaded all his equipment into it and locked it up with the intention of keeping it for his return. It ran out of registration, so there it has sat with his photography stuff all piled in the back."

They reached the garage. Peter unlocked the roller door and they walked into the musty semi-darkness; and there it stood.

Frank smiled. *Bingo!* he thought.

******

It had been a long but productive day for Pekalski. He had notified the forensic team and now only had to wait to see if his suspicions were correct, to reassure himself that he had not lost his touch.

As he drove home, he thought, *If I can make a connection between Jon 'Protestor' Chamberlaine and Roger 'Developer' Sleighmen, I'll need to know who the middlemen were. Naturally, the Sleighmens would have connected with either a single operator or an organisation that took care of the rough stuff. Whoever did the drive-by on Laurie Lyall's house, sent Jon Chamberlaine his threatening letters and did away with his dog, would have had nothing to gain for themselves. They had to be in the employ of someone who would benefit from the development going ahead.*

Pekalski's home was empty when he drove into the garage under the old Queenslander. His wife had made it her career over her last three years to restore it to its original glory; then she had died at the age of forty-six. Frank was still struggling to come to terms with his loss. No one expects to drop dead from a cerebral aneurysm first thing in the morning, after a good night's sleep, but she did, and Frank had not been there to hold her as her spirit soared to eternity. *Whatever that may be*, he had thought.

He walked into his kitchen, removed a frozen meal from the freezer, and transferred it to the microwave. He had little appetite lately and he felt all his clothes becoming loose, *Well, that's a good thing, anyway.* He turned the TV on and watched the news. After a few minutes, he turned it off again. He realised he was not concentrating so he sat down at the kitchen table and opened his laptop.

One thing about this job. It keeps me real; I can go out and make contact with any number of people who are much worse off than I am, and it numbs the pain. Stay too busy to think. That was his advice to himself. Sometimes it worked.

Chapter Fifteen

Andrew opened his eyes to shafts of light coming from the window on the eastern wall of the bedroom. The low winter sun reminded him of the passage of days and the limited time left to him. A sense of melancholy spread from his head down to his toes, clouding his brain and bringing a great sense of weakness to his whole body. He looked at his partner, Danielle, and she slowly opened her eyes and smiled at him. He had no smile to return, just a deep sigh; one of sadness and even regret, clouded in a haze of retrospection that he allowed to swamp him as he turned away and pulled the covers over his head.

"Do you have to go back today? You really aren't ready, you know." She slipped her arm around his waist and buried her face in his back, drawing in the soft warmth of him and filing it away for the interminable nights alone. Danielle was a strong person, not afraid to live alone, but, for all the comfort of the home Andrew provided and its idyllic setting on the hill above Victor Harbor, loving Andrew was making it more difficult.

"I miss you more, every time you go back to Adelaide. I know it's only an hour away but sometimes it seems it may as well be a million miles. The time we have together just isn't enough any longer."

Andrew turned in her arms and reached down, drawing her head on to his shoulder.

"Now I have to console David as well. He's so attached to you and really doesn't understand why his father has to go away so often," said Danielle.

Andrew allowed the silence to draw out while he gathered his thoughts. After a long sigh, he said, "I've been thinking a lot about us these last few days and I don't want to keep up this facade any longer either. It's just not worth it, to any of us. I had hoped to be financially independent enough to make it on my own in a couple of years. But now, it could all be in vain if we've lost everything. I think about what I've asked of you and how generous you've been, maybe all for nothing. It's greed, isn't it, to always want more? No matter how much I had, I only ever saw it as the beginning. I never imagined being like other men and just going to work for a wage. I always saw myself as my own boss, not having to answer to anyone else." Andrew rolled on to his back, blinking away the moisture gathering in the corners of his eyes. "Why did I think I was so different?"

Danielle reached up and held his face in her hands. "Anyone would react the way you did, Andrew, growing up in the shadow of Roger Sleighmen – remember how he treated your mum? Did he care that he was depriving you of her love? I wish you could find her now, I'm sure that so many pieces of your life would fall together."

Andrew nodded.

"I think you see now that what David and I want is you, not riches, or the things it brings. The thought of us living together, for always, is just amazing. Do you really mean you'll rethink your – our lives – can you?" Danielle had a pleading tone to her question.

"I can – and I will. I need to go back and sort out this present mess. I want to tell Dad about you and David, and he can either accept it or say goodbye to the last of his family. I don't understand his attitude or why he ever believed I should live my life the same way he has. I presume he wants me to carry on the Sleighmen dynasty, but he has a funny way of showing his belief in my abilities. He's certainly not a happy man and I'm bloody sick of his constant criticism and belittling, especially when it's in front of the staff. They say misery loves company and maybe that's his motivation."

"But love, he really has given you no other choice but to make a stand. To suggest you'd be disinherited if you married is absurd and no one should have to put up with the abuse you cop. I can't imagine what sort of life your mum had with him, but I'm sure she was better off without him."

"Yeah, I know you're right. I think I will attempt to find my mother when we're over this present disaster. I would have liked to have met with her as a success and introduce her to my beautiful family, but, success or not, it doesn't seem to be as important now. Time's running out and the longer I hang around Dad, the more I get caught up in his useless life. When I think about some of the corruption and illegal business he's been involved in, I wonder why none of it has ever caught up with us, and I say *us* because I haven't had the balls to say no to it."

"I really don't want to know about any of that," said Danielle, as she drew back in Andrew's arms and looked at him. "Imagine if we had to visit you in jail. No, get out, right now and consider yourself lucky to have survived."

David ran in and crawled up on the bed. He wriggled in between them and they both held him close. For the next half hour, they made plans, some short-term and some long-term and, by the time David had had enough cuddles, they had agreed on a new beginning, starting that day. After breakfast, Andrew contacted his father to say he would return later that evening. He spent his last few hours playing in the sun with David, hitting a ball around the grass, and throwing a Frisbee for the dog.

Danielle had overheard enough phone conversations to be aware that not all of the Sleighmen's business was strictly legal. She could see how this selfish, sometimes brutal man damaged parts of her partner. She wanted to shield both the men in her life from Roger and she would be truly happy if the business failed and they parted ways.

She did not make much as an artist, but it kept her busy and more doors were opening to her now that she had the luxury of painting almost full time. Danielle had no doubts about their future together. She had met her father-in law on several occasions, but as Andrew and Danielle had agreed, she could not tell Roger about her long-term relationship with his son nor even that he had a grandson. She just had to keep Roger Sleighmen out of her life.

******

Muriel Jacobs was waiting for her boss when he arrived at the office just after seven in the morning.

Without so much as a grunt in acknowledgement of her presence, Roger strode in, sat down behind his desk, and loosened his tie that had only been on half an hour.

"Is coffee made? Andrew got in last night and will be here soon. Do you still have those figures on hand?"

Muriel pointed to the tray, arranged on the small side table.

Roger helped himself, for which his assistant was grateful.

She indulged this man, but even she had her limitations, and she would not be afraid to tell him so.

He slopped coffee on his desk as he picked up the cup.

Muriel shuddered, but she switched her attention to the man who entered the office.

"Sorry to keep you waiting. Thought I could smell coffee." said Andrew, throwing his coat on to the stand and smiling at the other two as he poured himself a cup and walked up behind Muriel at her computer. He looked over her shoulder as she tapped on the keys at high speed. He raised his eyebrows and a smile began to spread across his face. "Is that for real? Are you sure? Is there any more?"

"I don't believe so, Mr. Sleighmen, but I'll keep trying. Most of this I found yesterday, with the help of someone who could be called an expert."

Roger Sleighmen's interest had been aroused. He walked over and stood next to Andrew. "What's this all about?" he asked.

"See these figures here?" Andrew pointed, and then traced his finger across a line of figures as he went on, "They represent an incomplete transfer of funds from one account to another. In other words, there is money that moved from our account to another holding account, where it was awaiting transfer to one of Thompsen's accounts. For some reason it was not completed, maybe accidentally. This has occurred on several occasions and it looks as though we can simply transfer it back."

"Not back, somewhere else!" Roger shouted. "We don't want the bastard having another go, do we?"

"Right, right, of course not." Andrew looked down at Muriel and nodded, giving her the go-ahead.

"Where to?"

"Any – fuckin – where," shouted Roger again. "Just get it away from him!"

"Hang on" Andrew put his hand up. "Thompsen would have details of all of our accounts. We'll need to open a new one – one that he's unaware of. Just a minute." Andrew dashed to his coat and took out his wallet. When he came back to the computer, he was reading out a set of numbers to Muriel and she was already punching them into the keyboard.

"Now, let's do the lot," he said to her, and for the next twenty minutes, Roger watched the pair work flat out, leaving him completely in the dark as to what was going on.

Finally, they both relaxed and breathed a sigh of relief.

"Can someone please tell me what's going on?" Roger's face was red with apprehension and excitement. He had no idea what had happened but he was hoping it was good.

"Okay, done!" Andrew walked over to a chair, then changed his mind, topped up his coffee and took the pot to Muriel's cup.

She smiled up at him and nodded.

"Well done," said Andrew. They both sipped their coffee while Roger blustered.

"We have just retrieved more than two million dollars," said Andrew. "Now, considering we've lost in excess of six million dollars I'm sure it doesn't sound that good, but it's a start. I don't know why Thompsen left those loose ends but I'm bloody glad he did. At least now, we have room to breathe and that investigator of yours has time to catch him up. We can do a part payment to the most demanding of our creditors, like the bank in Queensland – hold the wolves at bay for a time."

"So, who's the expert that showed you how to do all this?" The elder man looked at Muriel, accusingly.

"Someone trustworthy, I assure you, Mr. Sleighmen."

"I bloody hope so," said Roger, as he paced around the room.

"Please, please don't take offence at my father's stupidity and rudeness." Andrew walked around to face Muriel. "If he's incapable of acknowledging what you've just done, I'm not. I assure you I am very grateful. I can fully imagine how many hours you've put in to find this information. Again, thank you so much, Muriel."

"What about the bloody bank?" bellowed Roger. "How come they couldn't have seen this if it was so easy to find."

"It wasn't easy to find, Dad, and they would not have access to the information Muriel had."

"Well, where is it now? You moved it to another account. Was it Muriel's account?"

"No, of course it wasn't Muriel's account. It was one of mine."

"How come you have a separate account, one I know nothing about? One the accountant knows nothing about. Does this mean you have your whole separate stash?"

Andrew was fast losing patience. He took three, good deep breaths while the silence hung in the air. He sat down and Muriel stood and excused herself. The door closed behind her and Andrew tried to arrange his thoughts while his emotions raged through his body.

"The money was put in to the account of someone by the name of Danielle Hudson."

"Who?"

"Hudson. Danielle Hudson, my partner."

"Your what?"

"My partner of the past four years."

Roger stared at Andrew. Suddenly, he got up and left the room via the small door to the washroom.

Andrew sat tapping the chair arms and waiting to get on with his confession.

His father returned with a wet face and he took out his handkerchief and patted his face dry. He sat directly opposite his son and said in a quiet, but nonetheless intimidating voice, "What is this all about?"

"Four years ago, while I was on holidays, I met a beautiful girl and we established a very loving relationship. Since then, we've had a son. His name is David. We have a home at Victor Harbor. They live in almost seclusion, for fear of being discovered by anyone who might know you."

"So, you're married then? You've done the one thing I specifically forbade you to do."

"No, we're not married, much to my eternal shame for being such a spineless bastard. I've no idea how I could ever have allowed you to dictate my life to me for so long. I've been an absolute fool, but not for much longer. We're going to get married, with or without your blessing."

"Well, we can certainly agree that you are a fool, and now, you've just given her all our money – the money I've worked a lifetime for – money she'll marry you for. Well, she has it all now."

Roger was spitting, his face turning crimson by the second. "Jesus Christ," he gasped. He grabbed his chest, and slumped in the chair. Sweat poured from his face as he clutched his left arm.

Andrew knelt down and turned his father's face. "Dad! Dad!" he shouted.

From the office next door, Muriel heard the panic in Andrew's voice. She ran to Roger's office, took one look at her boss, and dashed to the phone and dialled 000. Between them, they rolled Roger over and checked his breathing and pulse.

"I can't get a thing," panicked Andrew.

"Hang on, I feel a pulse." Muriel held her boss's wrist lightly and looked at Andrew. "Yes, you try, don't press too hard."

Andrew began to shake his head then looked around for something to cover his father.

He grabbed his coat from the hook and gently laid it over him, then sat back on his heels, staring into space while the two of them waited for the ambulance.

"I'll go downstairs and direct them up," Muriel said, as she took off toward the elevator.

In a surprisingly short time, two Paramedics arrived. The staff had gathered in the room but fell back to allow clear access to Roger. One of the Paramedics quickly placed an oxygen mask over Roger's nose and mouth, while the other took his vital signs and then connected leads to his chest.

Within minutes, the ambulance had arrived at the hospital and Roger was rushed through the doors to Accident and Emergency. A doctor and a nurse began connecting him to the hospital monitoring equipment and oxygen supply as he transferred from one trolley to another – then the alarm sounded. Cardiac arrest! Staff responded from all directions. The defibrillator was activated.

"All clear!"

They waited for a response as the shock of the electric current jolted Roger's body. All eyes were on the monitor. They watched the flat line for a few seconds.

"All clear!"

Once again, the paddles were placed on Roger's chest. It jerked again as the current hit his body. Anxious eyes stared at the monitor.

"Sinus rhythm. He's back."

******

"He's had a myocardial infarct – a heart attack. He's conscious and, believe it or not, he's even trying to speak. I bet he's trying to give orders. He'll be complaining about the service next, but seriously, love, there's really no way of telling which way he'll go at this point." Andrew had stepped outside and was speaking to Danielle on his mobile phone. "I've been told by his physician that Dad was very lucky to have had such prompt medical attention, but despite that, the next few days will be critical. He said that this may just be a warning and he may still have another attack. They're keeping him in coronary care so we really can't relax yet."

"And how are you holding up?"

"I'm fine. I'll hang around here for the time being, but there is something I need to mention now. If you should check your bank account, don't think you've won Lotto. I've transferred two million dollars there – just for safe keeping for the time being."

"You've what?"

"Don't worry, it's our money, and the reason it's in your account is because it can be held there safely until I open a new account. I had no choice at the time and I'll tell you all about it tomorrow. Honest, don't be afraid, we've done nothing illegal. We had to park that money there for safekeeping. And I know I can trust you, my love." Andrew almost smiled.

"I'll be thinking of you, Andrew. If there's any change, please let me know and I'll come straight over."

"Thank you, my darling. Good night. Kiss David for me." He hung up.

Chapter Sixteen

"Yes, Mr. Sleighmen, we have the go ahead from the land council. They're satisfied that everything of interest to them has been removed and your property was not a burial site. They believe there probably was one nearby but the remains found there had been buried in a pile, by a person, or persons unknown. The police investigation of the area is also complete and the remains of the Caucasian man have been removed, of course. You can recommence the development after today," Stephen Brigges, the Sleighmen's Brisbane solicitor, explained to Andrew.

Andrew had just stepped out of his car. He stood at the door leading from the garage into the house he and his father shared. He had been at the hospital for a whole day's vigil at his father's bedside. The call had been unexpected. "Thanks for the call, Stephen. I really appreciate the effort you've put in on this. I'll be in touch – speak to you soon." He closed the lid on his mobile and pumped his clenched fist in the air with an accompanying, "Yesssss!"

Andrew walked in to the kitchen and found Danielle at the gigantic stove, stirring the contents of a large copper pot. Danielle and David had come up from Victor Harbor after Andrew had called and said he needed them to be with him.

Danielle wiped a wisp of hair away from her eye and held out her arms. She encircled Andrew's waist as he took her head and kissed her gently.

"Hi, love," he said, as he stepped back. "God, what a day."

"How is he tonight?" Danielle asked.

"The proverbial 'critical but stable condition', as they're so fond of saying. No, really, that's how he is. There's no change, – he just lies there, breathing in and out, fluid dripping into his arm, fighting hard. It's just a waiting game now."

"Oh darling, I'm so sorry." Danielle walked toward him with her arms out. They stood together, feeling the total comfort of acceptance and understanding. "I'm really sorry, Andrew. I know we've both been critical of him, but I guess when something like this happens, it does tend to make you, if not more understanding, then at least more accepting of his faults."

"Ah, I don't know that I've got to that stage, love. I feel sorry for him, I suppose, but probably no more sorry than I would for anyone else in his position." Andrew paused, then smiled and said, "Anyhow, do you want to hear some good news?"

"Sure."

"Our solicitor in Brisbane rang just as I got home. The ban's been lifted on the Keeala Resort extension. There's been some skulduggery over there, excuse the pun. There were old Aboriginal bones there all right, but they'd come from somewhere else and had recent Caucasian bones mixed in with them. There's an investigation going on but we're in the clear."

"So what happens now? Do you just recommence work on the development?"

"Sort of. Now that we have some money, we can make a bank repayment and get them to advance enough for the next stage. I have Power of Attorney to act for Dad, but there will be some legal requirements to fulfil first."

Andrew turned and looked around. "Did you find the media room?"

"I did, yes, and David is sitting up there in your father's recliner, like a king. I hope you don't mind."

"Of course not. This house is your house; you treat it as if you were home. There's a cleaning couple, come Monday and Friday. They do all the washing and ironing and cleaning, so you'll see them tomorrow and the cook will be here in the morning. I'll be gone early in the morning so just tell her what you want done. She'll shop and prepare meals, usually for several days, but you arrange it however you like. If you'd rather do the cooking, just tell her to ring me and we'll work something out."

Danielle stood there with her mouth open. "You know, living in that beautiful house in Victor Harbor, with all the bills taken care of, was a lot for me to get used to. But what will I do here? This is decadent, unbelievable."

"Why don't you pick up some art supplies? Right now, you have a pretty healthy bank balance. You might as well use it." He smiled and looked lovingly at the mother of his son.

"Andrew, that's exactly what I'll do. There's so much inspiration here. The light is different and the ocean is always changing. I could paint all day. Oh well, if it wasn't for David, of course," she said soberly.

"Why don't you do a deal with the cook? She's a nice person and I bet she would rather look after David than shop and cook. We can eat out or get takeaway, in fact that may be preferable. Look, make any arrangement you like with Katie, she's cool and you can get stuff in just for David and then I can bring something home for us. That's what Dad and I did before we employed Katie."

"Okay, leave it to me. I'm already having some ideas. Now, sit down and we'll have a peaceful meal – no talk about anything negative. Let's have some wine first and then we'll eat."

Andrew poured two glasses of a Sauvignon Blanc, gave one to Danielle, and took his into the media room where David sat. His son was staring at the giant screen, smiling at 'The Cars' movie and looking like he had always lived there.

"How's it goin' mate?" said Andrew, as he put his glass on a coffee table.

"Dad!" David jumped down and ran to his father.

Andrew picked him up and threw him above his head. He knew he would never again live away from this boy.

"I love you, son."

David hugged his father and squeezed his neck. Andrew carried David to the kitchen. He retrieved his wine and ate his meal with David on his lap, tickling him and talking rubbish.

"I can see there will have to be some new rules around here," said Danielle. The idyllic scene that played itself out was uninterrupted until bedtime when David refused to go to bed and Danielle had to exert the usual discipline. Finally, Andrew and Danielle sat quietly in the lounge, ready to get serious about the matters at hand.

"I'll have to go back to Brisbane this week. I have to go to the bank: set up a temporary agreement. I have a meeting with the private investigator Dad employed to track Thompsen down. We'll have no General Manager soon, as Neale Simpkins has resigned. Mind you, now that Dad is out of the picture and we look like re-starting, I have the feeling he may have second thoughts. I'll wait and see what happens there. Then there's all the usual business. I have to say, Muriel Jacobs has been great. She's really stepped into the breach. While I've been at Dad's bedside, she's just taken over. She really knows her business. I can't say how impressed I am."

"Have you told her?"

"I haven't had a chance. You can see how the phone hasn't stopped and I get no peace at home."

"True, but why don't you pick up the phone now and speak to her?"

"Yes, you're right." He scrolled to find her number and connected. Muriel answered almost immediately and Andrew got straight to the point. "I wanted to ask you if you would consider the position of General Manager, temporarily; until we have a board meeting and until you find out if you like the job." Andrew smiled. "Right. Meet me in my office at ten tomorrow, let's talk details. And put your thinking cap on because I need lots of inspiration. You know how much trouble we are in and I need all the help I can get. Great. Thank you, Muriel."

He hung up and turned to Danielle. "How come you know so much?"

"You haven't even scratched the surface yet. You should see me when I really get going."

They embraced and walked arm-in-arm to bed. That night became one of the unforgettable ones. Bonds were made that would last forever.

******

The following morning, Muriel and Andrew were a few minutes into their meeting when a call from the hospital interrupted their discussion.

"Yes. Thank you." David put the phone down. "Dad's not improving. I'll have to go there later."

"Certainly. I understand your position, Mr. Sleighmen, I'll continue with your instructions."

"Please, Muriel, call me Andrew. We've gone way past the niceties; I can't tell you how much I appreciate your input. I see you as a lifesaver right now. Don't stop. I need someone I can trust so I can get on with all the other stuff."

"I understand, and thank you." Muriel stood and turned to leave. "I hope all goes well in Brisbane. I'll keep in touch and don't worry about things here. It's okay."

"I believe it is."

They made eye contact and both knew the trust that was implicit.

******

"As I explained yesterday, your father's odds on improvement are lessened by his general condition. He is obese and has emphysema and his liver is only partly functional. Did he make an advance health directive?"

"What's that?" Andrew asked the doctor.

"A legal document containing your father's wishes if a situation like this should occur."

"No, not that I know of. My father certainly never mentioned it. He didn't like to think of himself as anything but 'in charge'. I'm sure he wouldn't consider the possibility of that much vulnerability – of being mortal. I can, however, make decisions regarding our business because I'm an equal partner. Are there more decisions to make now?"

"Not really, Andrew. As next of kin, you may be asked to make a decision about continuing life-sustaining measures, or ceasing them, if that situation should arise."

"When could that be?"

"Well, he is holding his own now. Let's just take it one day at a time. Could you please check with your father's solicitor about an Advanced Health Directive?"

"Yes, I'll contact him as soon as I get back to the office. Thank you for spelling it out for me, Doctor, I appreciate it."

Andrew went back to the office and began making calls to his Adelaide solicitor and some of his father's oldest friends, of which there were few. He also wanted to check his father's will was in order, to make sure of the process to follow should his father not pull through.

Later that day, he sat in his office chair and allowed his life with his father to play out before him. He acknowledged that, in his own strange way, his father had probably loved him, not that he had ever told Andrew so. Andrew reasoned that for his father to have done so would have been interpreted by him as a sign of weakness, of softness. So many painful memories welled up. Andrew found negativity overcame him that prevented him from smiling, even inwardly, at any memory concerning his father. Now, all he wanted was for it to be over, to begin a life with Danielle and David, and run his life in a way that did not make him feel ashamed. Most of all, he wanted David to be proud of him and never feel the resentment Andrew had harboured toward his own father.

Andrew's next phone contact was with Stephen Brigges to line up a possible new start for the Queensland development. After having given Brigges an update on the current situation, he said, "As you know, we've had a long-standing association with our bankers. They're going to play a crucial role in the resurrection of this project. We'll see if our loyalty over the years means anything. Perhaps this sounds a little extreme to you but I feel banking has become far more impersonal over the last few years; institutionalised thinking and computerised number-crunching are now the driving forces in making any decisions. Well, I'm going to put the bank to the test. I'll keep you posted."

Andrew rang his contact at the bank and made an appointment for a meeting at which he hoped to negotiate a rescue deal. The money they had recovered was not nearly enough to cover their present debts but he must convince his bankers that it was in everyone's interest to go ahead with the Keeala Resort development. The company expected to make a good return on its investment and surely the bank would be able to see that, Andrew reasoned.

He had his hand ready to punch in his next number when his new secretary transferred a call to him.

"A Detective Pekalski on the line, sir."

"Hello, Detective, how can I help you?" He listened while Pekalski explained that a current case involved an investigation into the background of a man called Jon Chamberlaine.

"This man was a major protestor against the development of the first stage of the Keeala Resort. He disappeared in very unusual circumstances and now his remains have been uncovered in the exhumation of aboriginal bones, about which you are aware."

"Yes." Andrew began to tremble. *So that's where he ended up.*

"I would appreciate it if you could make time to see me, Mr. Sleighmen. I'd like to see any records you have about the clearing and excavation of the first site, conducted about three years ago, I believe."

Andrew considered the detective's request and tried to grasp its significance. After several seconds, he replied, "I don't know if there is anything that would be of interest to you, Detective, but I'll look it up. I expect to be in Brisbane early tomorrow."

"Good, see you at say, ten, at your office. Is that convenient?"

"Yes, okay, see you tomorrow." They disconnected.

Andrew sat and cast his mind back to the time they were having a lot of trouble with CARP and other protestors at the start of their development. Karl Simmens had been recommended to him as the man to organise a response to the protests. He had contacted Simmens who had not only made the problem of Chamberlaine go away but had also taken care of indigenous bones that had been unearthed by one of the excavators. Fortunately, the operator had told Maxwell's supervisor about the find, and it had never been reported to police.

Simmens had dealt with all their interference problems, and, at the time, was considered expensive at $5000. However, now that Andrew had seen how much trouble the bones had caused them eventually, he wondered if it had not been cheap. His mind was racing, seeking answers, trying to make sense of what had been happening.

If those bones had simply been buried over the other side of the lake, did Simmens do it or had he delegated the job to one of his associates? Wouldn't Simmens have spoken up when the excavation of the other side began, if he knew they would be unearthed again? So... who did the job and who killed Jon Chamberlaine?

The discovery of the bones, coming on top of their financial problems and now the uncertainty about Roger, was almost overwhelming to Andrew. He sat in his chair while his phone rang; he realised this could mean the end of his family as well, if he was charged with the murder of Jon Chamberlaine. When his secretary looked in, she found him sitting lost in thought, deaf to the insistent buzz of the phone, unaware even of his secretary's concerned gaze. She made a quick exit and wondered if this was normal and whether she should tell someone. She decided to say nothing and get on with her work.

Danielle found Andrew to be especially vague that evening. She packed an overnight bag for him and put David to bed early. She had no idea what had changed but, like his secretary, decided to let him have some space. The next morning, at six o'clock, he flew out of Adelaide.

Chapter Seventeen

Frank Pekalski replaced the phone and wondered if he had imagined a defensive tone in Andrew Sleighmen's response to his call. He knew from experience that many people had that as a natural reaction when speaking to an officer of the law, but he judged Andrew Sleighmen to have been a little hesitant, even nervous, during the brief exchange. The reality of Sleighmen's state of mind however, would have to wait for further probing during the interview the next day; for now, other matters needed Pekalski's attention.

The detective opened a document on his laptop and scrolled down a contact list, selected a number, dialled on his landline and waited. Five rings later, the other party answered. Pekalski introduced himself and, courteously but succinctly, stated the reason for his call. He arranged a meeting later that afternoon.

*****

"I wish we knew more about the place ourselves," said Jim Watersen. "It would help us with the local politics and there's plenty of that in a place like this, I can assure you. Look, Detective, I'm sorry; we're probably not going to be able to be of much assistance to you, certainly not in respect to the history of the place. Wouldn't you agree, Di?"

Di Watersen nodded, paused, and then said, "We may be able to help with some names to follow up though, Detective."

"Please, please, call me Frank. May I drop the Mr. and Mrs. Watersen and call you Jim and Di?"

"Of course," affirmed Jim with a smile. He continued, "Di and I will be only too happy to help in any other way we can and her suggestion is a good one. You may wish to interview some of the residents; the majority of them have been here since the resort opened. Everyone here seems pretty open and happy to talk; sometimes you can't shut them up," Jim laughed. Pekalski nodded with a reciprocating smile.

"I'll give you a few names," Di chipped in. "Even in the short time we've been here, there are some residents whom I couldn't help noticing seem to be fairly knowledgeable about the goings-on in the resort."

Pekalski accepted a short list of names and house numbers from Di. "Thank you very much. I'll pursue these right now."

A short time later, Pekalski sat on a leather recliner, sipping green tea from a delicate, fine-bone china cup. Opposite him, on a matching two-seater lounge, sat his hosts, both sitting forward and giving Pekalski their full attention.

"We chose our home off-plan, so were able to watch it going up and, since we were both retired, I must say we often made a nuisance of ourselves on the building site." Harold Smith grinned at his partner, Robert, and reminded him of the time before they moved in at the resort. "I recall we seemed to spend half our waking hours watching the construction, and taking great interest in the progress of our own little house."

These men were the first on the list given to Pekalski. Di had described them to Pekalski as the font of all local knowledge. 'And they don't exaggerate, like some we know around here. I'm sure you can trust any information they give you, Frank,' she had said, confidently.

Harold continued, "I was unaware of anything being discovered in the excavation, but there was a time when the whole site was out of bounds to anyone except the workers. This, I believe, was to comply with safety regulations, which is fair enough I guess, but I do remember a lot of excitement over the protestors. Then, one day, the protests and confrontation stopped. We never heard or saw any sign of dissent again until this new development; now it's all flared up once more. You know, Detective, there are things going on around here that aren't easy to explain. I can't give you a picture, unfortunately, but Robert and I have a sense of a world within a world – if you know what I mean."

"I'm afraid I haven't a clue what you mean, Mr. Smith, can you be more explicit?"

"Afraid not. There are several shady characters hanging about, but no, I can see that won't help you. Forget all that; let's just say we'll keep our ear to the ground in future."

"Thank you. I'd appreciate that. Here's my card."

They all shook hands and went to the door when Robert grabbed his partner's sleeve and nodded to the gardener as he came along the path.

"There's one of them now, Detective." Harold spoke quietly to Frank and nodded as Kevin walked by, wheeling a barrow and smiling at them all. "One of the suspicious ones, I mean."

"I see. Why suspicious?"

"Sneaky, lazy. Keeps his head down and appears at the strangest times, in the oddest of places. He is a man with something to hide. Mark my words."

"I see. Well, I'll keep my eye on him too. Thanks again for the chat."

He waved as he walked away and was aware of curtains parting ever so slightly in some of the surrounding units. *I think I'm beginning to see what Harold was saying about the sense of ... what, menace? Maybe.* He picked up his pace and hurried back to his car.

Just as he drove away, he sighted the area managers. They were driving toward the salesman's office. He stared at them as they passed him. *Another odd pair. Perhaps this place is haunted – by all the indigenous dead.* Then he had to smile.

******

The next morning, Frank Pekalski arrived at Andrew Sleighmen's office twenty minutes early. "I'm sorry, Detective Pekalski, but Mr. Sleighmen has not arrived. He is on his way from the airport and should be here in a few minutes."

"That's fine, no problems."

"Could I get you a coffee, tea?"

"Thanks, coffee, black."

As Pekalski sipped the aromatic crema from the top of his coffee, he began to mull over the case. His instinct told him the Sleighmens were guilty as hell; of what, he was not sure, but someone had killed Jon Chamberlaine. That someone had left him to rot with the bones of someone's aboriginal ancestors. The only reason it had become known was the work associated with second development. Pekalski reasoned that if they had known the remains of a murdered man lay there they would have either removed them first or simply not done any excavation at that spot. He figured they would not be doing the dirty work themselves anyway, but no one else had an obvious motive to remove Chamberlaine, and get rid of a sacred site.

"Come in, Detective Pekalski." Andrew Sleighmen appeared from his office.

Pekalski was taken by surprise, but then realised that the office must have had a private entrance.

"Detective Frank Pekalski," he said, as he offered his hand. "Had a long flight?"

"Hi, Andrew Sleighmen – strong head-wind all the way," was the brusque reply. "Look, my father's in hospital and I've had my share of problems recently so I'd like to get this over as quickly as possible, if you don't mind. Take a seat."

"Of course. What's happened to your father, may I ask?"

"A heart attack."

Andrew did not expand further on his father's medical condition and spent the next half hour showing Pekalski plans and a few approval documents relating to the existing resort. The detective asked what Andrew may have thought were innocuous and unrelated questions and Pekalski saw that the other man was obviously bored and even frustrated with the line of questioning. He decided not to prolong the interview. Andrew Sleighmen would keep for another day. The interview concluded.

******

Andrew hurried to keep his appointment at the bank. By the time he arrived, he was feeling a lot better. He reasoned that from the type of questions the detective had asked they had nothing on him; it seemed no more than a fishing exercise, but he also knew he must find Karl Simmens and warn him about the present investigation.

Andrew was not very hungry, but thought he would pop into the Tavern for a light snack and maybe a beer. Maybe it would give him a chance to catch up with Simmens. Sitting at the bar, he started a conversation with an old bloke who had the look of being part of the furniture. Andrew bought him a beer. The man turned his head and tried to assess the face that made the offer.

"What d' yer want?"

"I'm looking for a man called Karl Simmens."

"Don't know 'im."

"Know who might?"

"Maybe."

Andrew took a card from his jacket pocket and slid it along the bar.

"I would express my gratitude to anyone helping me to get in touch with this man." He pulled the card back and took out a pen. He wrote the name, Karl Simmens, on the back of his personal card and then shoved it back again.

The other man picked it up and turned it over. "Cops lookin' for 'im?"

"Could be, if I don't warn him first."

"I'll see what I can do." He stared at Andrew who then took out a $50.00 note and handed that across as well.

Andrew got up and said quietly, "I'll be waiting to hear something."

******

In Adelaide, Muriel Jacobs had been busy. She picked up the phone to contact her boss and was rewarded by his immediate response.

"Your father is unchanged, but they say that is not good news. The doctor wants to speak to you today."

"I'll do that next," answered Andrew, a sharp edge to his voice. "What else."

"I've spoken to someone who would be willing to sell some money. Terms are, as would be expected, five points above bank rates."

She heard Andrew gasp and utter a barely muffled profanity. With reassurance in her voice she continued, "This party is trustworthy. I know him personally and there is no fear of the interest rate going up or his closing down on you. For a short term, I believe this is a workable option. I have a contact number here as well for you to speak to Hugh McManus. He's the private investigator your father employed to chase down Randell Thompsen."

"Give it to me."

Muriel obliged and then gave Andrew a quick rundown of the other business of interest to him.

Andrew, softening a little, smiled into the phone. "You certainly have some interesting contacts, Muriel, I'm sorry if I was a bit abrupt, I'm a little on edge. I'll talk to you tomorrow morning."

******

Pekalski had been able to track down most of Jon Chamber's movements for the last few days of his life. He had also found out that when Chamberlaine had arrived in Westbridge, he had not long before left a relationship and his partner had remarried. She, when Pekalski tracked her down, made it quite clear that she had not attempted to contact him since they had broken up. Pekalski discovered Chamber's mother was deceased and his father lived in a nursing home in England. His father suffered from advanced dementia and was not aware his son was dead, or even alive for that matter. While a few people had missed Jon Chamberlaine, there had not been much of an attempt to track him down, apart from the initial missing person report to the police. 'Out of sight, out of mind,' the detective had said to one of his colleagues. 'It's a sad indictment on today's society but a transient population creates little respect for the bonds of friendship. Most people are too busy to be bothered keeping tabs on anyone else. Unfortunately, that doesn't help me with my investigation.'

The detective had established, however, that Chamberlaine was last seen on an October night, four years back. He had eaten an evening meal at the local Chinese cafe and left about seven. No one had seen him since that night. A neighbour suggested he may have gone out again, as she heard a car reversing out of his driveway a little after eight o'clock that night.

Pekalski was glad he did not have any other pressing cases and he was able to spend the time he needed to follow trails and track down details with more time than usual. He was never concerned about working overtime anymore.

Nothing to go home to meant the freedom to follow leads without interruption. The detective continued his investigation.

******

After having inspected the recommencement of the earth works at Keeala Resort, Andrew was satisfied that it was all proceeding well. He headed back to his hotel room, went straight to the mini-bar, and selected a small bottle of white wine. He unscrewed the cap and poured the contents of the bottle into a standard issue, hotel glass. Not the sort of glass he was used to at home, thought Andrew, but it was at least a step up from drinking straight from the bottle. With his left hand, he placed the glass on the bedside cabinet. At the same time, he used his right thumb to hit a speed-dial number on his mobile. He waited, swore, and spent a few more seconds impatiently tapping his right foot. He then left a message on Hugh McManus's answering machine. He needed to set up a date to meet with him on his return to Adelaide.

Later that evening, Andrew lay on his hotel bed, his head propped up by two fluffy pillows. Half dozing and barely seeing or hearing snatches of the ten o'clock news, he was jolted out of his reverie by the sounds of his mobile phone vibrating on the bedside cabinet beside him.

"Hear you're having some problems, mate," were the first words he heard. "I hear you've been asking round for me – Karl Simmens."

"That's right, Karl. We need to talk. Tonight. Can I meet you?"

"Yeah, down in my ute. I'm parked opposite your building right now. I've got the green Falcon with the hard tonneau cover, not that heap-a-shit Crapperdore in front of me. Look out the window."

Andrew walked to the window and pulled the curtain. He saw the vehicle and nodded his acknowledgement. Serious though this encounter was, Andrew could not prevent a wry smile from curling his mouth. *The great Australian question,* Andrew thought, *Are you a Ford man, or a Holden man?*

"I'll drive down to the next block, park in McDonalds. You come along in five minutes." The phone went dead.

The hotel was on a corner block and Andrew saw the vehicle move off across the intersection and drive slowly down the street. He put on his sneakers and jacket and pulled the hood over his head. A minute later, he emerged from the hotel car park through a pedestrian entrance at the back and walked briskly along the narrow rear lane. He was sure no one had seen him leave. He reached the end of the laneway, cast his eyes up and down the side street and, satisfied, angled across the street to the intersection. The main drag was clear both ways and Andrew strode confidently towards the fast food outlet.

Andrew slipped into Karl's front seat. The cigarette smoke that filled the cabin nearly overpowered him. He turned down a window and took a breath.

"Don't know how you can breathe in here, mate."

Karl said nothing.

Andrew faced him and got straight to the point. "I need to know what happened to the protestor who disappeared, so conveniently, when we were doing the first development four years ago."

"A bit late to take an interest now, ain't it?"

"You're likely to benefit from this conversation more than I am, Simmens. A detective is on the trail of Jon Chamberlaine. Chamberlaine is the one I asked you to put the wind up when he was leading all the protests to the development. Now they've found his body – well, his skeleton. They were able to identify him from DNA, so now they know that we were the most likely to benefit from his disappearance."

"Don't need to be a genius to figure that out, mate," Karl put in.

"True, but we also would never have dug up the other area if we'd known the Aboriginal bones and a murder victim were buried there. Or at least, we may have taken other steps to have had them removed, if you get my drift."

"That's for fuckin' sure. I was the one help'n' to sell that property. I had no idea they were in the ground."

"Someone must know how they got there."

"Yeah, but the guy I hired for the job has now left the country. I know he and Chamberlaine met up in a car park at night, and I gather from info supplied to me, that there was a struggle and Chamberlaine was shot. An accident. The person in question made his own executive decision at that point and dumped the body with the bones that he was supposed to have removed. He didn't wait around to tell me how he had eliminated the problems. I made one of my rare errors of judgment – the guy was an amateur and freaked out when Chamberlaine died. I'd paid him up so he just took off, left the country and, I hear from people who knew him that he won't be coming back. I've also been told that he knows about the recent events and has definitely disappeared. So, problem solved, eh?"

"I doubt that, but the fact that he is gone does make it harder for the police investigation. How many other people know about all this?"

"Only two and they don't know one another and they both know different things. I, and now you, are the only ones that know what happened. And we're not talkin', are we?"

Andrew took his leave after telling Karl to keep him informed of any changes. The following day, he set the original plans in motion again, re-starting the development in earnest. He had enough money to go on with, but would only feel better when Randell Thompsen and his money were run to ground. *Strange,* he thought, *I'm already referring to it as my money.*

He returned to Adelaide in time to have a meal with his family, after a de-brief with Muriel on the phone.

Chapter Eighteen

When Andrew arrived at the hospital at eight-thirty the next morning, the doctor met him outside Roger's door. They could hear his gruff voice complaining to someone about his tea being cold. They were surprised to hear how alert he sounded.

"How are you going, Dad?"

"How the bloody hell do you think I'm going? For Christ's sake, a man could starve to death in this place."

"Not much chance of that," the doctor said to Andrew, sotto voce.

"Well, you're beginning to sound like your old self again, I see." Andrew walked to the only chair and sat down.

"I think I'll leave you two to get reacquainted," the doctor turned to go, but was pulled up short by Roger.

"Not so fast mate, I've got a few questions of you first." Roger pointed to the man's back as he raised his voice another few decibels.

The doctor turned, obviously unhappy, and unused to being spoken to in that particular manner. "How can I help you, Mr. Sleighmen?"

"Well first I want to know what else can be done for me while I stay here. I mean, what's the point. I can rest at home. At least there, I can get decent food and a drink if I want one." He looked at the doctor who was standing with his hands thrust deep into the pockets of his white coat.

"We will need to do a few more tests, of course. You will need some rehabilitation and also a consult with the dietician and a physiotherapist."

"Jesus Joyce, you must be joking. Just collect the blood today, will you? I'll skip the consults so write a programme for me, if you must, but let's get this show on the road."

The doctor stared at Roger, but said nothing. He looked at Andrew, and with a slight nod indicated, 'outside'.

Roger watched in silence as his son followed the doctor outside.

"I may have led a very sheltered life, sir, but I've never met the likes of your father before. I feel very inclined to go along with his wishes. The standard of care is obviously not to his liking here and that will continue to raise his blood pressure and put him at risk – not to mention the effect on the morale of every staff member he comes into contact with."

Andrew looked at the floor. This was not the first time his father had embarrassed him and he should have been used to it by now, but still he cringed and struggled for an answer.

The doctor waited, clicking the button on his pen with frustration.

Andrew shook his head and ran his fingers through his hair. He gave an exasperated sigh and looked at the doctor."Right," he said, "we should arrange for him to go home, today if possible. Dad can sign himself out and relieve you of all responsibility. It wouldn't be the first time he's done it." Andrew spoke quietly, but with determination. He knew his father would get his own way and it may as well be sooner, rather than later. His father could accept the risks and to hell with him.

******

Hugh McManus was a big man and not over talkative. He was surprised to find that Roger was not there to meet him.

"So you want to continue with the same agreement?" he asked Andrew.

"As you know I wasn't party to it, so please tell me what you both decided on." Andrew was now aware this man could tell him anything, but fortunately he had been around Roger long enough to guess what the terms might be.

McManus said they had agreed to a thousand dollars up front, and then a daily rate of expenses only, until Thompsen was located. "After that, the agreed fee was five thousand, with special allowances as listed and attached." He handed the agreement and attachments to Andrew for approval, who nodded as he read and then handed them back.

"Okay. Now tell me, what have you got so far?"

Andrew started to relax. He leaned back in his office chair and looked at this fifty-something, self-assured man. He was strong and lean of body; he spoke slowly and inspired confidence as he articulated his words. Andrew realised he was relaxing because of the way this man put him at his ease. He concentrated on the information.

"... so from there we tracked your associate to the Casino on the Gold Coast. He was not making any attempt to remain hidden and spent up big for a week." Andrew cringed at these words, but nodded for Hugh to continue.

"In June, he completely disappeared. Dropped out of sight. Evaporated. One day he was there, the next – poof! He had been booked into the Orient Hotel in Sydney and was at the gambling tables every night for a week. On a Monday morning, he booked out of that hotel and has not been seen since. You can have a look at the bank statement here." Hugh handed a copy of the Thompsen bank balance printout to Andrew.

"See those withdrawals there? They amount to.... "

"I see what they amount to." Andrew squinted as though they were hard to read. In reality, they were very hard for him to look at. Such figures as $10,000 and $25,000 in a single day. Then some days nothing at all. Then withdrawals for travel and accommodation and clothing. The man seemed to be a binge spender.

"What's his total expenditure so far?" Andrew knew he had to ask the question, but felt like covering his ears rather than hear the answer.

"Close to two million."

"Shit. We've got to stop this bastard. I know my father isn't always the best of men but he hasn't worked all his life just for that rotten prick to throw it all away. To just piss it down the drain and throw it away on gambling tables is too much."

McManus stood and strode around the office. He stopped in front of the plate glass window and looked out at the city skyline as he said, "The fact that nothing has been spent for a month makes me wonder if he's still alive."

That made Andrew look up. He almost had a smile on his face. "What do you mean?"

"Well, getting these figures here was tricky, but they are reliable. I can see where the rest of the money has gone, but don't know if it has remained there. It may be in safety deposit boxes, or someone else's name, or right where he directed it. That's what we're working on now. Cyber crime is for the professionals, as you will see when you get my friend's bill."

"What do you suggest we do now?" Andrew looked at the other man.

"Continue as we're going. We're making progress, and if something has slowed down the spending, so much the better. Don't be too distressed. I've seen worse cases than this and I feel confident we'll catch him. The only trouble is, with Thompsen ceasing to spend, the trail dries up. By the way, I meant to ask about your insurance."

"No, we were not insured against that type of misfortune. If only." Andrew shrugged and grimaced. "Keep me informed, I'm available anytime, as you know."

Andrew walked McManus to the office door. As the men shook hands, Andrew said, "My assistant, Muriel, has attended to changing all our accounts and is in my confidence if you can't get me."

Andrew could only sit and stare at the empty space after the investigator left. Having this news now was like the culmination of all his problems and more than he could handle. He put his head on his desk and groaned.

******

160

When Detective Pekalski went into the station on Friday morning, his superior was waiting for him.

"Come into my office," he said with a hard edge to his voice.

Pekalski followed him in and stood with his hands on his hips as though he was busy and not planning to stay long.

"Sit." A well-manicured index finger stabbed at one of the two visitor's chairs.

The detective sat. He waited while his boss shuffled papers around and answered the phone. Finally, call concluded, his superior asked, "How's the cold case going?"

"Well, I'm on to a few leads at the moment."

"But are you close to finding who murdered ... ," he looked at his notes, "Chamberlaine?"

"Getting there, sir." Pekalski wriggled in his seat. He had a feeling he knew where this was going and he did not like it. He looked straight ahead.

"You've got today and tomorrow, and then I need you to start a new case. We just don't have the manpower to spend all this time on past history."

Frank went to speak, but was cut short.

"Look Frank, I'd have liked to have seen this one cleaned up, but I have instructions from above that it's to be left to die."

"I see," said the detective. "Maybe I can follow it up in my spare time. Sometimes I get some of that on my way home from work."

"No, leave it, Frank! Like I said, up-above wants no more time spent on it, understand? Tidy up any loose ends and pick up this folder tomorrow afternoon." He indicated a folder tied with white tape.

Pekalski could not make out the case name on the small, upside-down, type-written label. "Whatever," Pekalski muttered under his breath. He sighed. If there was one thing he and most other detectives hated, it was being removed from an assignment before it reached a satisfactory conclusion. The Sleighmen case had been going reasonably well and Pekalski had put a lot of energy into it. He acknowledged that he still had many loose ends to tie together but he had some strong gut feelings about the matter. He felt confident of a result. Now, what the hell, the case was just going to be shut down. He did know it was pointless to argue, but he also knew he could not simply walk away from his hard work. He kept that to himself.

"What's this all about, then?" asked Pekalski. He pointed to the folder as he stood to leave.

"Tomorrow. I'll brief you when I get back from a meeting upstairs." The interview was over.

Rude bastard, Pekalski thought. *He must know it's not going to be that simple. Yes, he does, but he isn't saying. He knows I'll not walk away like that.*

Like the members of the Aboriginal Land Council, Pekalski had figured that the indigenous remains probably came from where the first stage of Keeala Resort now stood. It was most likely the bones had been removed and dumped in a pile on the other side of the lake. The person who had done this would probably not have expected them to be unearthed so soon, so perhaps he, or they, simply did not care. Whatever the answer, Pekalski thought it was more than a coincidence that a white man's bones had turned up in the same spot, only a few hundred metres from the site of the protest about the original development. Not only that, but the leader of the protest group apparently disappeared off the face of the earth at the time. People like the Sleighmens got rich at the expense of others, and maybe that expense was more than mere money, Pekalski thought. He could not let it go.

Later that day, Pekalski looked at his notebook where he had written the name, 'Karl Simmens'. He was definitely someone of extreme interest and was the next lead he planned to follow up.

Chapter Nineteen

Laurie Lyall drove into his garage and switched off the engine. He kept his hands on the steering wheel, as he stared vacantly at the instrument panel. *John Denver got it right – Some days are diamonds and some days are stones,* he thought, while he tried to create a smile. It would not come. He gave up, heaved himself out of the car, and went into the house.

"Hi, darl, late again. I expected you home at least an hour ago," Marian said. She walked up to her husband and kissed him lightly. She looked into his eyes and saw he looked exhausted. "You're dinner's ready, whenever you are."

"I don't have much of an appetite tonight, love."

He flopped down onto the lounge chair and looked at Marian.

"When I went in this morning I was all set to make a stand against the proposals Porterman made yesterday. I really thought I had the numbers to defeat him, but it looks like, once again, money talks and speaks loudest to the greediest. A couple of councillors, who I believed to be coming my way, defected at the crucial moment. I know they agree with me, in principle, regarding the public transport services to schools and the establishment of another two childcare centres. We discussed the fine detail and even came to an agreement about the most suitable location for the childcare centres. We had a lot of it nutted out when we went in yesterday. Then today they have done a complete reversal and voted both initiatives down in favour of one of Porterman's favourite schemes – the extension to the sports centre and the addition of another sports oval. We don't even fully use the ones we have now. But, he will have made promises to certain businessmen who have a vested interest in promoting various 'sports' activities which will directly benefit their own pockets.Corruption wins again!"

Laurie made a great sigh and sank further into the softness of the lounge.

"So, Colin Porterman paid these two to vote with him?"

"Of course, but I can't prove it. He's probably paid off others as well. I have no idea how many councillors are on the payroll."

"It's hard to believe, isn't it? We all want to live in the best possible community; we all have children that need an education and transport, but they base their priorities on getting more money for themselves. That is so frustrating."

Laurie stood and walked to the kitchen. He made an effort to eat his dinner, but after a few minutes, he pushed the plate away.

"Sorry, love, I appreciate the effort you've gone to, but I just can't do it justice. I think I'll go to bed." He kissed Marian on the forehead and walked toward the bedroom.

Marian turned to the dishes. When she finished, she found Laurie asleep on the lounge in front of the television.

"Hey, go off to bed you silly man," she said as she shook him, and he followed her to the bedroom.

As Marian prepared for bed, she remembered Laurie saying he could not understand how so many people in the community knew, or at least suspected, that Colin Porterman was a corrupt mayor, but still they voted for him. Was it lack of an alternative, Laurie had ventured, or did most people simply not care? Marian knew Laurie was determined to find the answer.

The next day, Laurie bade his wife goodbye with a smile, saying, "I don't know where it came from but I seem to have found something to live for, overnight." He laughed at the expression on Marian's face, "Don't worry love, I think you'll find I'll be alright."

He disappeared happily down the driveway and was deep in thought when he arrived at his office in the council chambers half an hour later.

"Can I see you for a minute, Laurie?" Rose popped her head around Laurie's door.

"Certainly, come in. How're you going Rose?"

"I have a little problem, as a matter of fact."

Rose took the seat in front of Laurie's desk. She crossed her chubby legs and composed her pretty features. A woman in her forties, she came from a Polish background and seemed to fit in well with the other councillors. Not the type to fuss over much about her appearance, she always managed to look good, although she dressed simply.

Laurie had observed when he first met Rose that she had a strong, determined personality. He thought she would probably not be easily intimidated.

"Do tell, how may I help you?" said Laurie.

"Laurie, I had a visit from Justine, this morning. She's Colin Porterman's assistant, as I'm sure you know."

Laurie nodded, then reached over and turned his phone to message bank as it rang.

Rose looked uncomfortable but continued. "She says that her boss has been making sexual advances toward her. I mean Colin."

Again, Laurie nodded and held Rose's eye contact. "Can you be any more specific?"

"She had mentioned this once before but I'm afraid I didn't take her too seriously. The way she dresses sometimes, well I don't think it's all that appropriate, for a place of business like this, I mean."

"I understand." Laurie listened.

"Last time, she said Colin always touched her when he walked past and usually made some smart remark, like maybe, 'How you going, 'sexy', or 'putting on a bit of weight there, love', and patting her backside. She said he often leaves a gift on her desk like flowers or chocolates, with a card attached, saying, 'I like my women cute'. She said at first she felt complimented but things have changed and now he is getting serious."

"How? In what way?" Laurie was listening very intently now.

"Recently he has asked her to have a drink with him after work. The first time she made an excuse and he accepted it, however he asked her again the day before yesterday and got very annoyed when she told him she was going straight home. He reminded her who pays the wages and how he expects his assistants to be loyal and available to him. Apparently, she got upset and started to cry, at which point he told her to shut up and go home. Now today, he has called her into his office and told her that he expects her to keep in confidence everything they talk about, and if she works overtime, she will be paid for it. He says he has a business meeting tonight and she has to attend. He also suggested that if that's not possible then he will be looking for a new assistant – one that is loyal and dependable."

Rose took a deep breath and looked at Laurie while shaking her head. They both knew what this business inferred and sat in silence, digesting the full connotations of the situation.

"How was Justine when she told you all this?"

"I'd say she was angry first, afraid of losing her job second, and determined not to put up with this harassment, third."

"I'd like you to ask her if she's prepared to talk to me about it. If so, come back to my office, the both of you, as soon as she's free to leave her post without Colin missing her."

"What's your plan?"

"I'm not sure, but we need to get something together before tonight. We now have a shot at exposing one of the most corrupt men in local government. Are you up for it?"

"You bet," Rose smiled. "I noticed he's always friendly with the young girls. Anyone my age, he completely ignores. Especially me, now he knows I usually support you. I have a mind to ask around. I wonder if Justine isn't the only one he has approached."

"Yes, I wonder about that too, but let's not telegraph our punches. We don't want to do a thing to arouse his suspicions before tonight. Please get Justine in here as soon as she's free."

"I will." Rose left, a spring in her step.

Laurie laced his fingers under his chin and totally immersed his thoughts in a plan.

******

A few minutes after one, Rose knocked on Laurie's door. "Okay to come in?" she asked. "I have Justine with me."

"Sure, come in and close the door."

Laurie rose from his seat and beckoned the two women to take a seat.

"How are you Justine?" he asked.

Laurie took in Justine's anxious demeanour, her attractive figure and long, blond hair. He thought she wore more makeup than she needed and again her dress was too short for his liking.

She attempted a smile as she looked at Laurie and sat down. "Rose said you would help me with the situation I have with Mr. Porterman."

"Can you tell me the story, from the beginning?"

Justine nodded and pulled her dress down toward her knees as she launched into a tale, even more interesting than the one Rose had told him. Obviously, she was making an effort to remember dates and details, now that she had someone genuinely interested.

"So, that's very interesting. I believe you are aware that you may be a victim of sexual harassment in the workplace. Have you told anyone about this?"

"Well, I haven't told my parents. I'm sure they'd be telling me to resign. That's something I'd rather not do. I see this as an important part of my career path and I'm sure not jumping off it unless I have to."

"Good, I agree. What I think you should do is see a lawyer – someone who can advise you of your rights and what procedure you should take. The trouble is, you may only have tonight to get the evidence you need to prove your story. Who knows if he'll try again, or whether he'll get wind of your complaints. I think you should strike now. It will take courage to pull this off, Justine. Do you think you're up to it?"

"What would I have to do?"

"Agree to go out tonight. Play it cool, I mean, don't act any more anxious than you were previously. Act intimidated, as though you believe you may lose your job if you don't go along with him. At the same time, give him a little encouragement, a giggle here and there; act as if you are warming to the idea. Do you have a smart mobile phone?"

Justine put hers on the desk and turned it on.

"Good. Does it record?"

She demonstrated her skill by recording while Laurie spoke in a conversational tone. "How's this?" she asked. She played back the last couple of minutes of Laurie's words.

"That's great," he said. "Now, what we're looking to record is his acknowledgement of who he is. You will need to ask him a question that clarifies he is the Mayor. For example, you might say, 'When did you get elected, or, do you like being the Mayor of Westbridge?' Know what I mean?"

"I do."

"Allow him to incriminate himself as much as you like, but do not encourage him in such a way as to infer you were a willing participant in the evening. Say as little as possible and allow him to dig his own grave." Laurie leaned forward to emphasise his point.

"I do get it, and don't worry, I know what we're after. What about going home, how will I get away from him? He might try to force me to go with him."

"I think the best plan will be for you to get an urgent phone call, after you have your evidence. Let's say I ring you about eight, saying I'll pick you up out front of the restaurant. Tell Colin your mum is ill and your dad is picking you up to go home and then go with her to the hospital. Porterman won't be able to stop you leaving and I'll have a friend, posing as your dad, to pick you up outside. It also gives you an excuse for being away tomorrow. I'll organise an appointment with a good lawyer and try to get you to see him tomorrow morning. I'll make that call now. If you want me to come with you tomorrow, I'm happy to do so."

"Yes, I'd appreciate that very much. By the way, I've discussed this business with a close friend of mine. Do you think I should speak to her and tell her to be quiet?"

"For the time being, definitely. If you know of anyone else who's been a subject of the Mayor's amorous advances, let me know. We'll leave that until after you've had a meeting with your lawyer. He'll give us some clues as to how we can discover just how far-ranging Mr. Casanova's activities have extended."

"So, I leave work tonight with Mr. Porterman. I put my phone on the table in the restaurant, saying my mother isn't well and I'm concerned in case she rings. I record our conversation and get him to say who he is. After that, I mostly let him talk. Well that won't be hard; he is his own favourite subject. Finally, I receive a call from my dad to say he'll pick me up outside the restaurant so I can go home and be with my mum at the hospital. I'll tell him not to expect me in tomorrow. I'll drive off with your friend and he'll take me to your place. You'll take me home after we've documented the facts for the lawyer who we'll hopefully see tomorrow."

"Wonderful!" Laurie and Rose both laughed and shook Justine's hand. "If you perform that well tonight we will hang this bloke out to dry."

Justine turned and looked at Laurie with a quizzical expression. "So you don't like him then?"

"No, Justine, I do not like our boss any more than you do and I believe this place would be much better if he were not here. It's not something I would advertise, but since we are working together to right an injustice, then it's appropriate that you know how I feel. It would be fitting that he brought himself down in this way and saved the community a lot of money and time. So, until tonight, good luck, and don't hesitate to call me if you have a problem. Remember you don't have to go through with this, you can abort the mission any time."

They both smiled and Rose followed Justine back to their respective workstations.

Chapter Twenty

Darkness was closing in when Frank Pekalski drove into the resort. The managers had closed the office for the night so he knocked on the door of their residence. Di answered and ushered the detective into the lounge. Jim joined them.

"Sorry to disturb you so late, but my time here is limited and I wanted to catch you. I wanted to ask you if you had ever had any dealings with a man by the name of Simmens, Karl Simmens."

They both shook their heads.

"Hmmm. That's a bit of a bummer. I'm trying to follow a lead in relation to the murder of Jon Chamberlaine."

"Sorry, I've never heard of him," said Jim. "How's the case going?"

"I wish I could say it was going well, but I'm afraid I've come up against a few obstacles, not the least of which is time. Can you make some discreet enquiries please? Anyone who knows this man, I'd love to talk to them."

Di looked at the detective and wondered how his wife felt about his working such long hours. *Such a pleasant, honest sort of man. He gives me the feeling he'd be very reliable and strong,* she thought.

They said goodbye and he went off in his car.

"Just when I thought I had something," he muttered, as he drove home to an empty house again.

******

The affairs of the resort were a bit of a mystery to the new managers. On an otherwise uneventful day, Jim found himself adjudicating a dispute between two neighbours, Richard White and Tony Miller. He had been asked to intervene in a disagreement between the two after their neighbour, Jessie Thornton, heard them quarrelling. Her home stood between theirs, and she often found herself in the middle of insults and bad language flung from one side to the other.

As Jim approached the area where the two men lived, he recalled that Robert and Harold had explained how White and Miller had been enemies long before they had unwittingly ended up as near neighbours in the resort. Their feud stretched back to when they had lived in the same Queensland country town and had been at loggerheads as business rivals for years. Later, their children had forged a link between the two families by marrying, only to sever the ties later through an acrimonious divorce. How both men and their wives managed to choose the same place to retire to is a mystery, but they continued their feud and entertained themselves and the other residents with their colourful bickering about anything and everything.

On this occasion, the dispute was about garbage bins. White said the other had switched them, because he, White, cleaned his regularly, and Miller did not, and now he, White, had a dirty bin.

Unbelievable, thought Jim, as he checked both bins.

"I hope this settles your dispute," Jim said to the two men, as he painted their respective unit numbers on the lids of both bins. "Now, there can be no doubt about the ownership of each bin. Agreed?"

Jim knew from experience that the microcosm of society contained within the walls of the resort could expose every type of behaviour. The meek, the strong, the eccentric, the mean, the givers, the takers, the joiners, the recluses, the drinkers, the wowsers – this disparate group was no different to the outside community; it was just more noticeable in the relatively confined surroundings of the resort. Jim had just never seen it so sharply demonstrated in any of the resorts or villages he had managed before.

He was slowly coming to know more of the residents. He knew who liked to swim every day in the heated pool, and who attended the gym. He noted the bowlers and the tennis players. He particularly appreciated the strength of the social committee and the various other groups that existed for the enjoyment and personal development of anyone who wanted to participate. Jim had commented to Di that Jessie Thornton was involved in the Palliative Care Group, which had formed to assist anyone who was chronically or terminally ill.

"Such a worthwhile cause, Jessie is a good hearted soul," he had commented. "Personally, I'm glad we were invited to join the music appreciation group. It's a nice way to get to know like-minded people."

Despite their settling in and making friends, there continued to be an undercurrent that was impossible to trace. Most people did not notice it, but those that did, found it hard to explain. The salesperson, Matthew Weatherlee, seemed to attract odd friends and was often evasive when Jim met him. Jim was determined to discover what was amiss. *But not today,* he thought.

******

The work on the other side of the lake had recommenced. This time there was a genuine urgency to get the buildings up and sold. Since most of them were off-plan sales, there was no way the Sleighmens could minimise their commitment, or downgrade in any way, what they were offering. Everything had to be of the highest standard and finished to the buyer's expectations. The work lagged, but if the contractors kept to the present pace, they would come in close to the nominated completion date.

Maxwells gave Charlie Gibbs the sack. They did not want independent-thinking operators who could not follow orders. The land clearing was complete, and the ground works for the foundations, plumbing, and cement pouring was underway. Andrew Sleighmen kept in touch with his foreman on a daily basis and was satisfied that if the building was finished on their new time schedule, he would be able to pay back a large part of his overdraft to the bank in Queensland. He knew they were extending him more than he had expected and the pressure was on to deliver on time.

******

The private investigator, Hugh McManus, was late checking in with Andrew; however, he finally turned up at the

Sleighmen building in Adelaide on a cold, August, Monday morning.

Andrew stood when the investigator knocked. Andrew pointed to a chair. "So, what do you have for me?" he asked.

McManus walked into his office and made himself comfortable. He pulled a note pad from his pocket and flipped back the cover. He spoke slowly and quietly, allowing every word to sink in. "It seems to me your friend is smarter than I first gave him credit for. Led us on a merry chase, he has. But he has no idea he's being pursued, and that's to our advantage."

Andrew leaned back in his chair and quickly followed with, "He's not my friend and how can you be so sure he doesn't know you're on his tail?"

"Because he acts like a confident man and moves money around at will. He no longer goes to the trouble to transfer and withdraw funds in his original convoluted system. In the beginning, it was hard to trace where money was coming and going, but now, we can almost watch him think, and fortunately, for you that is, he's stopped spending. By the look of it, he seems to be over his initial spending spree and is now laying up money for his old age. My concern now is that he'll hide a stash where even we can't get access to it."

"Can you tell me how much money is left?"

"Sure – well, approximately anyhow. Take a look at this spreadsheet."

"Yeah, I see. Well, Hugh, with what we've been able to recover already, together with knowing the whereabouts of substantially more, maybe it won't be as bad as we first thought."

"Agreed. If we can get this money back, you'll probably have lost around two million. I know it's not to be sneezed at, but it's a damn sight better than six million."

Andrew still looked serious, but with a lighter expression than he had begun with. With a half-hearted chuckle, he asked, "So, now what?"

McManus leaned back in his chair and created a pyramid with his fingers. A slow smile spread across his face. "We set a trap for our friend," he said.

Andrew began to feel excited and his eyes widened as he waited for the investigator to continue.

"We will need the cooperation of the police if we want to have this man prosecuted of course – the fraud squad in particular,"

"I see." Andrew waited anxiously for the man to continue.

"I know a few people here at headquarters in Adelaide and I've made contact with the man who'll help me set things up." McManus took a long breath and left Andrew to hang on his last words while he considered some detail of his plan. "We have the cooperation of the bank and we plan to request Mr. Thompsen come in to the bank to sign certain forms in relation to his internet banking. We will probably say the original form he signed was incorrect or some such thing. The account will be frozen if they don't get his signature. Then we wait. When he comes in, we grab him. End of story."

"Sounds too easy. Will it really be that simple?"

"Probably not, but that's our plan and one that has worked for the cops before. I'll need you to come and meet the head honcho of the Fraud Squad. You'll have to make a statement, then, the quicker we move the better. What do you say?"

Andrew was immediately alert when the investigator suggested he meet with the police. He was as wary as any other guilty man was, and had no liking for police stations. He even wondered for a moment if he was being set-up. He sighed deeply and shook his head to banish any such foolish thoughts.

"Sure, count me in. whatever I can do, absolutely."

"Good. Time for me to work out the fine detail. I'll get back to you as soon as I've arranged for you to go into the station." McManus stood and lazily extended his hand. A tiny smile curled the side of his mouth.

After the investigator had left, Andrew sat and allowed his mind to drift. So much had happened in the past six months, he wondered if he would ever have a peaceful life.

Chapter Twenty-One

Colin Porterman stood back and held the restaurant door open for his assistant. "It's a shame the others can't join us after all, there was so much I wanted to discuss with them. But we all have to eat, so we might as well enjoy ourselves. I have to say, my dear, it's great to have your company and I appreciate your making the effort to be here." The words spewed from the Mayor's lips, almost falling over themselves in their haste to put Justine at her ease.

She smiled up at him and slipped the phone from her bag to her hand as they waited to be shown to their table. She pressed 'Record'.

When the waiter had left them with a menu each, Justine placed the phone next to the centrepiece on the table, out of Porterman's line of vision.

"I hope you don't mind the phone but my mum hasn't been well and I'd like to be available if she needs me."

As they sat quietly, studying the mouth-watering descriptions on the menu, Justine noticed her foot tapping nervously under the table. She put her hand down to steady it.

Porterman noticed Justine's nervousness and said, "Relax, my dear. There's no call to be afraid of me. I'll look after you, as I have always, at work. You know you were my personal choice of all the applicants for the job of Mayor's Assistant. I've been very happy with your work, most of the time. There's room for improvement, of course, but you stick with me and you'll go far. I could see you doing one of the advanced administrative courses at TAFE, at the council's expense, next year, if you're so minded."

Justine looked up at her boss, as if she needed confirmation of his last statement. As she did so, she reached for her water glass and accidentally knocked it over. In her haste to avoid it dripping on her lap, she upset the table and the cutlery and the rest of the table paraphernalia fell noisily to the floor. She and Porterman both stood and watched the mess unfold in slow motion before them. Justine saw he was not happy.

His lips squeezed together and he stepped back, waving to a waiter.

Suddenly, Justine remembered her phone and stooped to grab it with one hand, before it too, was wet. At the same moment, Porterman pulled her by the other hand, away from the chaos, suggesting it was not their place to clean up their own mess.

A waiter arrived, and then another. They righted the table and quickly picked up the things off the floor.

Justine looked up at her boss and could see he was angry. She realised he obviously did not like the attention they were attracting and she watched warily as he huffed and muttered, looking around as if for an escape.

Finally, the waiters held the chairs for the pair at the freshly laid table. One also held the phone out to Porterman.

"That's not mine," he said. He did not try to hide his irritation.

The waiter went to put the phone back on the table. Justine leaned over and quickly snatched it from his hand.

"You won't go far if you're always so bloody clumsy," growled Porterman.

"I'm sorry, Mr. Porterman," she said. "What sort of a clumsy idiot am I? Can you believe that? I'm so sorry, Mr. Porterman." She reached out and took Porterman's hand.

He looked into her eyes.

Smarmy bugger, she thought, as she looked down coyly.

The redness finally began to subside from his face. He appeared to be trying to come to a decision.

"Let's not let a little thing like an upset table spoil our dinner," said Porterman, as he waved the waiter back. They finally sat looking at one another, while the wine was placed in a bucket at Porterman's elbow. He poured, and they looked deeply into each other's eyes. Justine began to think she liked this game; she was really getting into the swing of it.

"So, Mr. Porterman?"

"Please, please call me Colin, away from the office." He smiled lasciviously.

"Yes, well, Colin, do you really think I could do that advanced administrative course you mentioned, before I became overwhelmed and upset the table." She laughed as she leaned across the table and reached for his hand again.

"Of course, why not?"

"What are the requirements for me to be eligible? I suppose there's access to information like that on a web site?"

"Not important, Justine. If you wish to do any of the courses available, my recommendation is all that's required. As I said to you before, I'm happy to reward loyalty in my staff. You have potential and you're a hard worker. I've had my eye on you for some time. Now, no more talk of business – we're here to enjoy our dinner. To you!" He raised his wine glass in a toast and grinned. "Is there anything else you would like, my dear?"

She looked into his eyes, and said, "I think I have everything, thank you. By the way, Colin, I've never been to the Winthrop Hotel before. It's very nicely appointed, isn't it? Do you come here often?"

"Well, as a matter of fact, Justine, I do. I come so often I have a regular booking for my favourite room, the Honeymoon Suite. Speaking of which, Justine, it's still early. Why don't you come up to my room after we've finished our meal? I'll order some champagne. We can have a few drinks and get to know each other a bit better, if you get my drift?"

"Do you mean, if I scratch your back, you'll scratch mine, Colin, if you get my drift?"

"Precisely, Justine. I knew you'd see the career opportunities that would present themselves if you were especially nice to me. You're a quick learner, Justine."

Justine lifted her glass slowly and reciprocated Porterman's toast. She did her best to smile but it was non-committal.

Porterman's unspoken response said so much more.

"Colin, I just have to powder my nose." Justine excused herself and disappeared into the ladies. She was pleased to find it empty, and she tested her recording.

"Bloody perfect!" she said aloud, grinned from ear to ear, and quickly punched in Laurie's number. "I think I have all I need, Laurie," she said quickly, when he answered.

Laurie confirmed he would make the call to her in a couple of minutes and she put her phone back into her purse. She returned to the table.

Porterman took her hand and squeezed it as she sat down.

Her phone rang. The conversation was short and one-sided. Justine disconnected, but then hit the 'Record' key on the phone and placed it on the table next to her handbag.

"I'm so sorry, Colin, I'm going to have to leave early. Unfortunately, my mother is quite sick and she has to go to hospital," Justine said, as she stood and picked up her handbag and mobile phone.

Porterman grabbed her by the wrist.

"Surely your father can do that. You can't run off and leave me by myself, now." His brow furrowed and his mouth showed a hard line of determination.

"I really am so sorry. I don't know if I'll be able to get into work tomorrow. I'll ring in as soon as I know."

"If this is what you call loyalty, then we now know where your priorities lie." He sat sullenly, staring up at the girl. "Don't be surprised if opportunities go to someone else. You can't expect me to put your case forward when you aren't prepared to do anything for yourself – or me."

Justine nodded and gently extricated her hand from his grasp. "I do think I know where I stand Mr. Porterman. My family is more important to me than my job. Do what you must."

She picked up her bag, turned and walked to the restaurant door, then, looking over her shoulder, she noticed her phone still on the table. Justine almost tripped over in her haste to return to the table. She lunged and grabbed the phone.

The Mayor looked away as the girl walked out.

"Bloody stupid little bitch!" He spat the words out.

******

Laurie Lyall did not have to look far to find a lawyer with an open mind. His brother-in-law, Chris Young, said he would be happy to see Laurie and Justine the next morning.

"Come in. Take a seat," said the solicitor. He smiled at his clients as they sat, and he opened a file on his computer. "So, this is interesting, isn't it?" he said. "Our dear friend, Colin Porterman, has finally left himself a little exposed. I would certainly be interested to know if he's approached any other young ladies in the workplace."

Laurie answered. "I had planned to investigate that, Chris. I wanted to see what you had to say about Justine's case first though. I realise that once I begin to ask around, it'll get back to him in a flash. I expect Justine will be looking for a job as soon as he hears we're asking around."

"Let him give her the sack – more grist for the mill. 'Girl loses job when she confronts local politician.' Sounds an alright headline to me," Chris said, with a grin.

"Hmmm. What about her job. Should she look for another?"

"There could be a compensation case if Justine chooses to pursue that aspect, but those things take time. Living at home makes it a little easier. Let's wait and see how things go – one step at a time."

Chris got all the information he needed and said they had enough to accuse Colin Porterman of sexual harassment, but proving it was another step. "The more cases you can discover, the stronger Justine's claim will be," he said.

"So," said Laurie, "we go back today and Justine goes into work and apologises for being absent for the morning. We document his response, record it even. This afternoon, Rose and I will question as many employees as possible. If we uncover anyone with a supporting story to tell, we'll get back to you, ASAP."

"Right. Let's nail this bugger, once and for all. I'll be as delighted as you to see him hung out to dry." Chris wished them good luck and saw Laurie and Justine out.

After a delightful vegetarian lunch the pair sat at a little restaurant table at Southbank and Justine watched Laurie's expressions as he explained his plan to interview other girls at the council chambers. The sun shone softly and the light river breeze brought a mix of river and city aromas on it.

"Do you know what I mean?" he was asking. She realised she had not heard a thing he said. He was looking like a hero to the young girl and he inspired her.

"Oh, yes, yes I do." She nodded her head vigorously and then lapsed into watchful silence again.

"Must be time we got back to the job. Shall we go?" He stood, and his eyes followed her as she slowly made her way, absentmindedly, toward the door.

Chapter Twenty-Two

"You wanted to see me, boss?" Pekalski closed the door of his superior's office.

"You picked up a suspect, name of Karl Simmens, in connection with the bones found in the Keeala Resort development case?"

"That's right; I have reason to believe..."

"You were told to leave it alone. How much more time have you been putting into this?"

"Just my own. I believe there's a murderer out there and I think I'm pretty close to catching him."

"You realise that the word to drop it came from the top. Even if you bring a fucking murderer in with a signed confession, he'll be out again in five minutes."

Pekalski slammed his fist down heavily on to the other man's desk. He leaned forward until he was centimetres from his boss's face.

"I used to have respect for you, you bloody wimp. What sort of a business are you running here? Who's paying your wages?"

The other man grabbed Pekalski by the front of his shirt.

"I don't give a shit what you think, Pekalski. I work for a living and you can just shut up about matters that are not your concern. If you were in my place you'd understand, but you're not."

"If being in your place means becoming as corrupt as the crims we're here to put behind bars, then you can stuff your job – right up your arse." Frank turned around and strode out of the office. He left the door open and the rest of the staff in the outer office stared after him.

A pall of silence fell over the room, shattered when the boss walked to the door and slammed it shut.

Frank Pekalski had never thought his boss was a crook. Even now, he had a nagging suspicion that the scene he had just left was in some way flawed. He arrived at his car and stopped as he put his fist on the door handle. He punched the car and then let his arm drop to his side as he turned and leaned against the vehicle. *What's going on? Who was it that threw the anchor out, and why?* He thought back to the day before yesterday. A reliable source had given him a tipoff. He followed it through and found Simmens in the bar, right where the bait had been dropped. He fed him the line he had prepared earlier and arrested him on the spot.

Bringing Simmens in for questioning had brought him no joy. He learnt nothing new and Simmens was smug. A professional, not intimidated, and was out again in a little over two hours. The detective knew he was on the right trail and that his arrest would get back to the Sleighmens. How much good it would do was very doubtful, especially now he knew he was treading on someone's toes and their priorities were more important than his. *Maybe I should go back to the boss and apologise. No, if he was going to let me into his confidence, he would have already. I'm on my own with this and that's that. I certainly won't be going in there again for a while*, he thought as he drove off.

******

Allen Sinclaire, the Sleighmen Group area manager, had cause to worry. It was his job to see that all drugs coming into the country, under consignment for the Noonans, found a safe home. The last shipment was late and there was a disturbance up line. He had no idea what the holdup was, or even if he had cause to worry. He walked into Jack Noonan's office and was a little intimidated, as usual.

"Sit. What's going on?"

"I wish I knew," Allen responded, palms raised, but trying to look confident.

"If you don't know, who the hell does?"

He shook his head. "You know better than I do how much can happen. I've done the usual checks and I believe the stuff left the base as always and then all I get is a blank after that. Maybe a rival gang intercepted it before it was loaded, or maybe it was knocked off coming here on the ship. All we can do is wait until we're contacted, and even then we're at their mercy, as you know."

"Not good enough. What about Aaron?"

Sinclaire nodded. "I haven't been able to make contact with him either. He knows he has to lie low whenever there's a glitch in the system. He's your man and he won't make contact until it's safe."

Jack nodded. "Okay, let me know if you hear anything."
He pressed his intercom and spoke to his secretary.

Allen had to conclude the interview was over so he
stood, mumbled his goodbye, and left.

Allen Sinclaire had worked for the Noonan brothers for
more than twenty years, and for their uncle before that. He
knew the business well enough and this situation had
occurred before. He thought through the details again. Aaron
was Norman Noonan's son, and had been Jack's apprentice
for most of his young life. He had no desire to go into politics
like his father. He was very good at what he did. He remained
in Asia under the guise of an international surfer and handled
the drug connections and deals. He had all his own contacts
and he had become indispensible to the business. He was
being groomed to take over from Jack when he retired. Allen
thought he would like to be out of the business by then. He
had no desire to answer to a boy of twenty.

Allen called into Keeala Resort on his way home. As
pre-arranged, he left a message in the mailbox of an empty
unit. Kevin would have to stall his customers, use up
whatever stash he had in reserve, until the next shipment
arrived. He knew Kevin would be pissed off; he hated losing
customers to the competition. *Fuck him,* he thought, as he
looked in the rear vision mirror and ran his hand through his
thinning hair. *Better take a little gift to the old girl, you
handsome bugger.* He smiled and accelerated into the traffic.

Georgeina awaited.

******

Karl Simmens rang Andrew Sleighmen on his mobile
phone.

"Make it brief, mate." Andrew resented this intrusion.

"A friendly warning. Cops picked me up in connection with the skeleton found on the development site. I gave them nothing and it's my suggestion to you that you sit tight. They can't prove a thing. The detective's just following a hunch and you're probably next in line for questioning, after me. Remember, the guy who did the deed is not in the country and you're the end of the line. Maybe they'll lose interest, but I wouldn't bet on it."

"Okay, thanks." He hung up. This was Andrew's greatest worry, aside from the loss of the money and the demise of his business. "Jesus, Joyce, what else can go wrong?" he said, through clenched teeth.

Simmens was thinking about disappearing for a while, but he was not sure if the timing was right. It would look like he was avoiding something and he could see the detective involved would probably not let go easily. He decided to hang in there, bluff it out. Maybe he could even lead the cop up a few garden paths. Maybe.

******

The alluring aroma of freshly brewed coffee wafted up to Pekalski's nostrils as he sat at his kitchen table. Much as he loved the taste and smell, he often wondered whether it was the few minute's distraction in the making of it, which gave him the most satisfaction. It offered a rare opportunity to take a few moments of respite from the pressure of the job, some quiet thinking time. Pekalski sipped more and stared at nothing in particular. He wondered if it was time to let the Sleighmen case go. He did not believe the son had murdered Jon Chamberlaine but he was certain Andrew Sleighmen knew who had. Simmens had a perfect alibi, being interstate during that time, so if it was not him, then who?

Someone at work, someone near or at the top of the force, wanted to pull the plug on the investigation and Frank could end up out of a job if he continued the way he was going. Chamberlaine had no family to grieve for him. Maybe that was why Pekalski felt he, if no one else, should seek justice for the dead man. *Ah, what the hell*. Frank took his coffee into the living room and flicked on the television. He just wanted to get the case out of his mind for a while. He decided to be absorbed in the weather channel.

Chapter Twenty-Three

Justine steeled herself as she made her way back to the office. Chris had explained to her that she might be in for quite a deal of criticism and even aggressive behaviour from her boss, once he became aware that she was bringing a charge against him. The solicitor had insisted she talk to her parents that evening as well. She would definitely need their support.

As she walked down the corridor, shouting from the Mayor's office startled her. A young girl burst from the doorway of his office and ran past her. Justine stood frozen for a moment, wondering whether to go forward or back. Then the big man appeared, framed by the doorway with the sun behind him, slanting through his window. *He looks like a monster from hell*, she thought, and turned to leave.

"Where the hell have you been?" he shouted at her.

She did not answer – just stood and stared. Porterman took two steps toward her and she turned to run.

He stopped, and said, "For God's sake, where the hell do you think you're going?"

Bolstered by the recent support she had received, Justine decided to stand her ground. She flicked her hair back over her shoulder and looked her boss in the eye. "I'm not coming to work to be abused by you or anyone else. What happened to that girl?"

Porterman could now see how the past few moments would look to an audience. He burst into a raucous laugh and turned back to his office. He held the door open and waved his assistant in behind him, "Come on, Miss Hunter." The 'Miss Hunter' was blatantly emphasised. He closed the door behind her and pointed to a chair. "How's your mother?"

"Better today, thank you," she answered icily, as she sat on the edge of the seat.

"What's the problem, my dear? You look a little tense."

"What happened to the girl who just ran out of here?"

"Useless. Couldn't find an elephant in a shithouse. That's what happens when you go off and leave me to the mercy of incompetents, Miss Hunter. Are you back now?"

Justine hesitated before answering with, "Yes, sir. I'm ready to work. I did ring in this morning. My mother's home again now."

"Right, well, back to work then, shall we. I've left a pile of correspondence on your desk. I hope that idiot girl they sent over hasn't made a mess of it. I'm behind now, but that can't be helped."

He stood and held the door open again for Justine, something he was not in the habit of doing, ever.

The phone rang as Justine returned to her desk.

"I heard there was a bit of noise going on at your end of the building. Everything alright?" It was Laurie.

"Yes, okay now, thanks Laurie, just someone being chastised for incompetence, I think. Doesn't appear to be too serious. Thanks for the call, Laurie." Justine hung up and looked at the work on her desk. She sighed and wondered if this job was worth so much trouble. *Yeah*, she thought, *it'll be worth it to see that bastard brought down.*

Much later that day, Justine was still in front of her computer, as her workmate's desks were tidied and vacated for the night. The Mayor came out of his office and stood for a few moments, watching her at her workstation. He came up and stood behind her.

"I don't expect you to work overtime because you came in late today. Everyone needs their rest. How about a quick drink on the way home?"

"No thank you, sir," Justine replied, as she turned to face him. "I want to be with my mother and I've decided to make it a policy not to fraternise with work mates."

"Have you now?" His eyes widened as he stepped back. "Since when was I a workmate? I think you have a short memory. Last night we agreed that I required a loyal assistant, one who was agreeable to do an advanced administrative course at no expense to herself." He took a somewhat more aggressive stance in front of her, so that she had to look up at him. "Don't come in here to work and lay down the law to me, young lady."

The girl gathered up her notes and piled them on the end of her desk. She turned her computer off then picked up her mobile phone, which just happened to be on the record position.

"Good night, Mr. Porterman." Justine gathered her bag and walked toward the glass doors.

"I haven't finished with you yet, Miss Hunter." He watched as she ignored him and disappeared down the corridor.

"Nor I you, you slimy old bastard," she said.

******

Laurie made a call to his brother-in-law. "Why don't you come to dinner tonight and we can talk in comfort. I'm sure Marian will be happy to see you."

"Sure, love to, mate. You'd better ring her first though. I don't want to be the cause of you and my sister divorcing."

" Yeah, I'll do that. Say about six?"

They sat in the lounge after dinner. The kids were in bed.

"Anything happen when Justine went back to work this afternoon, Laurie?"

"Well, I heard the big man had the temp in tears and running from the building, but Justine said all was okay after she appeared on the scene. I'll talk to her tomorrow and keep tabs on the situation."

"Laurie, you know this issue will cause quite an upset when the media get hold of it. Even if unproven, an accusation of sexual harassment against the fine upstanding leader of our community is really going to bring out the knives." Chris rubbed his chin, lips pursed.

"I know. If he goes down, a lot of the support he's gathered over the years will go with him. His influence in the business community is significant and there's some very big money invested in keeping him where he is. How should we go about questioning the other girls tomorrow?"

"Be quick. Between yourself and Rose, speak to as many as you can because you need to go to the police with your complaint in the afternoon. By then, the man will have wind of what's going on and will probably try to shut you down." Chris handed a slip of paper to Laurie. "This is the name of the inspector you should ask to speak to at the cop shop. Tell him I told you to ask for him. You can call me from there if it's appropriate, otherwise I'll come on board when they interview Justine."

"You know, Laurie, you've really got yourself in at the deep end this time. Don't get me wrong, I think you're doing the right thing and I admire you for it, but it won't be easy and some of the vested interests can play rough. You've already experienced a drive-by shooting and, I must say, Marian and the kids will be caught up in it all as well." Chris leaned over and kept his voice low. "That's what really worries me, Laurie. It's another reason to get the police involved tomorrow. Any moves Porterman makes now will only dig himself in deeper, but that doesn't account for his friends. Do you think Marian and the kids should leave town for a while?"

"Possibly," said Laurie.

"Can't do any harm and it might free your mind up. You're going to have enough to focus on without worrying about them. Why don't I drive them to Sydney? They can spend a few weeks with Mum and Dad; take some school work with them and so on."

Laurie frowned and sat on the edge of his chair. "I'll think about it tonight. I realise if they go they should do it soon." Laurie ran his hand through his hair a couple of times, then said, "No, I think you're right Chris." He stood and walked to the door. "You there, Marian?" he asked.

She answered from the kitchen, and then joined them while they discussed the plan.

Chapter Twenty-Four

Getting everything set up had taken longer than expected. It was September, and Hugh McManus liaised between the investigating police detective, the bank, and Andrew. Internet fraud was an expanding business and many computer hackers did not want to work in conjunction with the police. For that matter, most of them did not wish to even be identified by the police. McManus had his own professionals, but he needed more. He knew they would get a shot at Randell Thompsen, but when they did, it had to be right.

Andrew introduced Hugh to Muriel Jacobs's hacker friend. Andrew said, "Hugh, this is 'our friend'. He located the embezzler and the missing Sleighmen money in the first place, and he'll work with you in an anonymous capacity. No names, no pack drill, eh?"

They had finetuned the course taken by the rogue accountant and could now see exactly how he operated. They had to take great care he did not become aware they were so close to him. The police were finally ready to go and a tentative date was set to have Thompsen come into the bank and sign forms, so he could access his money.

The bank manager contacted Thompsen on his pre-paid mobile phone.

The rogue accountant had been careful and knew the authorities would have difficulty tracing his whereabouts through that mobile, not that he thought they would ever make the connection between his real identity and the fake one he had used to open the account. He agreed to come in the next day at midday. He was wary of anyone taking an interest in his money, but the bank had made it clear there was a small oversight, just a formality really, on their part and they unfortunately could not allow him to access his money until they once again sighted his ID and had signatures on a couple of extra documents. Only two people in the bank, apart from the manager, were aware of the set up, and they were not told until an hour before the time.

A female police officer had replaced the woman at the front desk and a male officer sat in the foyer. He appeared engrossed in a brochure extolling the bank's customer friendly mortgage rates. Another police officer slowly completed a deposit slip at a bench and checked the BSB's on a couple of cheques supplied by the bank. Hugh McManus sat at a customer service table and discussed the latest deposit interest rates with an unsuspecting bank service officer. He had insisted on taking a role so he could remain involved. Andrew suspected Hugh was excited by the prospect of the final sting and simply could not stay away. Andrew too would have liked to have been a fly on the wall when they finally nabbed Thompsen, but he could not afford the risk of Thompsen seeing him anywhere near the bank.

Thompsen did not show up. They waited all afternoon. He did not arrive. Everyone was disappointed but, more than that, they wondered if he knew he was being set up.

"Fortunately, the police can think like criminals," said Hugh to Andrew, when they met in his office that evening. "They think he was just testing the situation and he'll wander in at a time of his own choosing."

"Does that mean we have to keep everything in place until he just turns up?" Andrew's concern was apparent.

"It does. We can't afford to contact him again. We'd look too keen. So we just wait."

He came the next morning, a few minutes before opening time. McManus waited fourth in line at the front door and became aware of someone joining the queue behind him. He focused on the reflections from the shining glass entrance doors and slightly shifted his stance to the right. The movement was enough to expose the face behind his in the reflection. McManus recognised Thompsen and gagged on his silent curse.

There were no police in sight. McManus looked around and felt for his mobile phone in his pocket. The movement of staff inside the glass doors of the bank suggested they would open any moment. Hugh could feel the man's breath on his neck as the push from behind gave a slight surge.

McManus felt his pulse go up a notch. He imagined himself turning around and grabbing the man and maybe twisting his arm up his back in a lock, or pushing him to his knees against the wall and ordering a bystander to call 000. But he hesitated. *What if he overpowers me and runs off down the street? What if he's got a gun and shoots me where I stand? No, I need to stall until the police arrive.*

The doors opened. McManus entered and went to a brochure stand where he selected a leaflet explaining the bank's Privacy Policy. He watched Thompsen walk in slowly. The accountant looked around as he joined the two customers in front of him in the queue at the service desk. McManus took cover behind the brochure stand and punched the inspector's phone number into his mobile.

The police officer answered immediately. "Sorry, Hugh, we're caught in a traffic jam, a vehicle accident. I'll get someone to you from the other direction. Try to stall the bugger. Don't do anything heroic, scared men can be dangerous."

The private investigator moved to the side of the foyer and knocked on the manager's door. The man looked through the clear glass panel and recognised the private investigator. He mouthed, 'Come in.' McManus quickly told him what was happening outside.

"Okay, we must stall this man, Hugh. Why don't you place yourself at the front door and I'll serve him."

"Right, if he tries to leave before the cops get here, I'll grab him on his way out," Hugh said to the manager's back, as he followed him to the office door.

The manager cautioned, "Don't follow me when I leave the office; you go back the way you came and sit on a chair in the foyer, close to the front door. Remember, I can lock all the doors in a second with my remote control if he looks like getting away. Please don't put yourself at risk unnecessarily." The manager turned to look sternly at the PI but the investigator had already rushed off in the other direction.

The bank manager casually approached the female service officer at a reception desk and whispered, "I want you to leave the desk. Invite the customer you're serving into a private booth. I'm replacing you. We've a 313 situation." The service officer nodded that she understood the code and followed the instructions without question.

"Mrs. Johnson, perhaps we'll have more privacy in an interview booth. Would you like to follow me?" she asked.

The manager seated himself at the desk and continued to process the customer ahead of Thompsen. Finally, Thompsen was at the reception desk and he explained how he had been asked to come in to sign forms. He pulled out his identification and slid it across the marble-topped desk.

"Thanks, Mr. ... er ... Fairburn. By the way, I'm Brian Mulcahy, the manager. I apologise for the delay this morning. It seems the early birds are out in force today. If you could follow me, we'll use my office." The manager beckoned to a staffer behind the teller's cages and asked her to take over at the reception desk.

Mulcahy opened his office door. "Please, after you, Mr. Fairburn. Take a seat. I'll see about processing this right away. Look, all my staff is flat out with this opening rush. It'll probably be quicker for me to grab the appropriate forms myself. Please, bear with me. I'll only be a couple of minutes." The manager left his office. He shut the door as he went.

The manager found McManus, semi-concealed behind an indoor potted plant near the front door.

"Where the hell are the police? I can't stall this guy indefinitely. I also can't lock everybody in here with him – he represents too much of a risk."

McManus pulled his phone out again and rang the inspector.

The manager turned and went back to his office. He opened the door, only to be confronted by Thompsen, alias Fairburn, making a hasty exit.

Thompsen pushed the manager to the floor and raced toward the front door. Hugh McManus was still in conversation with the police and did not see the man race past him until he had almost reached the door. At the same moment, the manager reached for the emergency shutdown switch. McManus realised his inattention may have serious consequences and he made an almighty lunge for the man making his escape through the quickly narrowing gap at the bank's entrance. The doors locked behind Thompsen while McManus beat his fists on the doors inside the bank. Thompsen dashed across the footpath in a couple of strides and ran straight into the path of a police car. The squealing tyres of the vehicle almost drowned out the sickening thud as Thompsen's body hit the bonnet first, then smashed the windscreen before rolling limply onto the roadway. The police car came to rest angled across the carriageway.

A moment later, the inspector arrived. Already, a crowd gathered around the scene of the accident. The bank's doors remained locked.

******

"It doesn't seem right somehow, celebrating the success of Randell's capture, while he lies in a bed in critical care." Andrew Sleighmen handed beaded glasses of champagne to Danielle, Roger, and Hugh McManus. They sat on the plush, studded leather chairs in the lounge of Roger Sleighmen's palatial home. Andrew joined them and raised his glass.

"To a successful conclusion," he said.

The other three raised their celebratory drinks.

Andrew continued, "I even feel sorry for the man who thought he'd benefit or be happy as a result of stealing our money. What could've driven him to such extremes? In all the years I've known Randell, he was only ever nice. A little tense and mostly serious, but that was the nature of his job; not exactly a light-hearted occupation. I know he was divorced and I think there were a couple of kids in the background. I really should know more about him."

Hugh said, "Perhaps we all get so involved in our own struggles to survive that we often are blind to the needs of others. When I met you, Roger, I judged you were not someone to suffer fools lightly, not one to compromise either. However, in the business world we breed them tough, eh, or one simply doesn't survive."

"You're right about that," said Andrew. He took Danielle's hand in his, as she reached across the coffee table to him. He looked at her and smiled. "I have the feeling things are going to improve from now on," he said.

"It may be that your father and I will actually like one another, eventually," said Danielle, looking at Roger.

Roger stood up and knocked his glass of wine onto the floor. He opened his mouth to speak, but closed it again. For the second time in his life, he was at a loss for words. On first sight of his grandson the previous day, he had also done nothing but stare, mouth agape. He strode purposefully to the window and stared out. His hands clenched and his shoulders heaved.

McManus attempted to diffuse the tension in the room. "So what are your plans, Roger? I guess you'll be out of action for a while, so I suppose Andrew will be holding the fort?" Hugh asked.

"Pig's arse! It's bad enough he installed his mistress and bastard son in my house while I was in hospital. If he thinks he's going to take control of my business, he's got another thing coming. I'm not done yet, not by a long shot."

"You mongrel, Roger!" said Danielle. She marched out of the room.

Hugh stood and cleared his throat, unable to hide his discomfort at Roger's behaviour. He said, "Time I went. I've a business to run, too. Thompsen's accident wasn't the conclusion we expected, or wanted, we can only wait now to see if the man recovers and let the law take its course. I'll see myself out."

Roger and Andrew were oblivious to the man's departure. They stood, eyeing each other.

Andrew spoke first. "It's time we had a very serious conversation and got a few things sorted out. I might be your son, but I'm also a man. This is going to be a man to man talk, not a father to son lecture."

Roger surprised his son by turning to his chair and flopping down. Whether he was tired or just resigned to the inevitable, Andrew did not know, but this was probably the only chance he was going to get to have his say. Andrew drew up a chair facing his father.

"Because of you, I have never known a mother. Because of you, I have no friends of my own, just as you have none. Because of you, I am a criminal and could go to prison for a very long time, simply for trying to please you. Because of you, I am unable to marry and make my children legitimate. Because of you, I am ashamed of myself. Is that what you intended for me? Are you really prepared to die knowing what you're leaving behind. Do you have any understanding at all what love is? Have you ever cared?"

Roger did not flinch. He sat and stared at Andrew. The only sound was the tick, tick, tick of a grandfather clock in the corner of the room. Silence hung ominously. Roger adjusted his position in the chair, crossed his arms, and sat shaking his head slowly as his chest heaved.

After a couple of minutes, Roger spoke, the vitriol barely disguised by his softly spoken words. "Boarding school – university – overseas travel – first class accommodation – lavish home and the best food, clothes and car money can buy. On top of that, access to opportunities and challenges to run a successful business and defeat your enemies." Roger stood up and stepped toward his son's chair. He could not restrain himself any longer. He leaned over him and pointed his finger into his face. "You ungrateful little prick." Roger spat the words. " I've given you everything a man could wish for and still you're not happy. I've sacrificed my own happiness and freedom since you were born, just for your benefit. This is the thanks I get, even now, when I should be getting care in a hospital, I'm here, looking after you." Roger turned and once again flopped on to his chair. Silence descended again.

"They're just things, Dad. Where was the love?"

"Get out. Take your gear, your car, and those two pieces of shit in there and get out of my life. I never want to see you again. Bugger off!" Roger turned his head so he could no longer look upon his son.

"I intend too, but before I go, I want my share. I haven't spent all these years working for you and being your lap dog, not to mention risking my life, for nothing. I have dependents now, and they will not go without while you still live and breathe."

"No. You leave as I said. That's it. This is not negotiable. You'll get not one red cent more from me, ever, I'll see to that."

Andrew shook his head slowly and chuckled. A smile spread across his face and he said, "I think you'll find I've not yet transferred the two million dollars retrieved by Muriel, back to the business account. You can see me in court. I'll look forward to getting on the stand and telling the world how you came by most of your money. I'd even go to prison myself, just for the pleasure of seeing you there." Andrew got up and started toward the door where Danielle had so recently exited.

Roger attempted to follow his son.

Andrew did not turn around. He did not hear his father make a muffled noise and fall back into the chair, nor did he see his father open his mouth and gasp like a fish, as an excruciating pain gripped his chest and rendered him speechless. Andrew slammed the door behind him.

Chapter Twenty-Five

It became clear to Detective Frank Pekalski that he was running a one-man race in his endeavours to find the murderer of Jon Chamberlaine. He was also aware he was falling into a hole of depression; a result of his self-imposed social isolation since the death of his wife. He had mourned her after she died, almost a year ago, but not sufficiently, and he had no wish to discuss his feelings with anyone. He delayed going home at night, as when he got there, he had very little appetite. He was suffering from insomnia as well. His dreams, when he did sleep, left him exhausted the next morning. He dreamed of constantly running away, then looking for his wife in a maze of buildings with endless steps and corridors.

It was springtime, October, when he woke in the middle of the night, sat up in bed and was aware his cheeks were wet with tears. He fell back to the pillow in exhaustion, threw his arm over his eyes, and sobbed quietly.

"No more, please, no more," he whispered.

He lay awake until he got up for work and then had to drag himself through the same old motions to start the day. Somewhere on the way to the police station, reality set in. He decided to let the Chamberlaine case drop. He was getting more than just opposition from his superiors. He finally realised that he had better take seriously, the order to stop investigating the case. He knew he could not bring Jon Chamberlaine back to life. *Let it be.* Frank wondered if a holiday might be what he needed, but then the thought of going somewhere, feeling miserable, could only make him worse. He would rather be miserable at home.

******

Karl Simmens had been in contact with certain men in the same line of business as himself and they had informed him police had called off the search for the murderer of Jon Chamberlaine. Simmens had never dropped his guard, but when he heard from the same sources that Chamberlaine's killer had come back into the country, his sense of unease began to grow again.

"What the hell does he think he's doing, coming back now? I don't care if he does stay in Western Australia, the cops can still trace him there," he said to his source.

"He ran out of money, he missed his family and he couldn't get a job. He decided it couldn't get much worse so he made the decision to return. I don't blame him. He can get a new identity and work here. There's no reason to think he'll have a problem."

"I think he's a bloody fool and he's putting us all at risk."

"Yeah, whatever Karl."

******

Allen Sinclaire had become used to worrying about the police. They were an ever-present threat to his happy existence, and suspicion of everyone was part of his natural defence mechanism. The drugs had still not landed. He went to the wharves to meet two shipments of artefacts and furniture, but both were devoid of their special cargo.

"This is not going to do anyone any good," he moaned to himself, as he drove back to Keeala Resort. Even Georgeina had failed to brighten his day with her mindless chatter and ongoing suggestions about how they could both do a better job. He left more and more resort business to her and even he had to admit, she had imagination and plenty of energy.

Allen drove around the resort, looking for Kevin. He found him with his feet up on a bench, smoking a cigarette.

"All right for some people. Taking it easy mate?"

Kevin was unperturbed and smiled at Allen. "One needs to rest when the opportunity arises, as you well know."

Cheeky bastard, thought Allen. "Well, I'm afraid I've got bad news again, son," he said.

"I'm definitely not your son, old man." Kevin always had the last word.

"Whatever. There's still nothing to give you. The shipment that came in today yielded absolutely nothing. Zilch. It was empty. Devoid of drugs."

"Keep your voice down," said Kevin, as he stood up and began to reassemble his gardening equipment. "If this continues for one more month, it'll finish me. We'll lose all our contacts and they won't come back, even when we have some gear for them."

"I know. I'll contact you as soon as anything changes."

Allen got back into his car and made his way to the sales office. He had to keep his eye on Matthew Weatherlee. He was the type who liked to operate independently, and that meant more vigilance for the area manager.

Matthew looked up as Allen entered. He nodded and ended his phone conversation. "What's up, Allen?"

Allen ignored Matthew and walked around the small room. He ran his hand over the pile of correspondence on the desk; mainly requests for pamphlets and information from would-be buyers. Matthew's eyes followed Allen as he realised they were playing one of the manager's many games. He remained silent and leaned back in his chair. Allen walked to the window and stood for a few seconds, then turned and walked out the door, slamming it as he went. Matthew shook his head and tried not to get angry, but could not help himself.

"What a dickhead," Matthew muttered.

******

If Jim and Diane knew about even half of the subversive activity going on in their own backyard, they would be horrified. Fortunately, they operated unencumbered by those facts and tonight they were going to enjoy a music appreciation evening at the home of Robert and Harold.

"You know they used to have an antique and old wares shop in Sydney?" said Di to Jim, as they changed for the evening.

"That so? Well, they both seem like fussy types. One can't imagine either of them driving a front end loader."

Di laughed. She began to wonder how the pair dealt so well with the criticism that some of their neighbours directed toward them.

"Do you think they hear what some people say about them?"

"They must, some of it is aimed directly at them. They've had their whole lives to get used to that attitude, but I do believe it would always hurt. I must say, I had little time for the idea of homosexuality before I met those two, but they're just the same as the rest of us. I really think people should mind their own business, including us."

"I guess so." Di checked her image in the long mirror. "You'll do," she said, "Let's go."

They made their way downstairs and along the pathway to the next block of houses. Tiny lights lit the paths and the cool night air was invigorating. Winter over, they were beginning to settle in and look forward to summer. They reached the house at the same moment as several other guests. Everyone was so friendly and welcoming, and soft chatter and laughter filled the air; they were all ready for a night filled with beautiful music.

Chapter Twenty-Six

Laurie Lyall moved quickly the day after his meeting with Chris Young, his lawyer brother-in-law. He and Rose were at work before anyone else and discussed their strategy. They wanted to interview as many women as possible before the Mayor heard about what they were doing. Gossip travelled like wildfire around that group of offices, so they needed to get as much information as they could before they were interrupted.

"We need to talk to the likes of Rebecca and Joanie in the secretary pool first. They'll be quick to tell us what they know, while others such as Elaine and Katherine may be hesitant to discuss such a sensitive matter with anyone. We'll leave the hardest until last and try to record them all. Of course, we'll have to tell them they are being recorded, and they'll have to agree, on the record," Rose said to Laurie. He nodded an acknowledgement.

They decided to go together. It would look more official with two, and Rose's presence would help with any gender imbalance.

"Hi, Rebecca, may we have a word with you?" asked Rose, as she saw the young secretary walk up the front steps. Rebecca looked surprised and even more wary when they asked her to go into Laurie's office.

"What's wrong?"

Laurie said, "We have reason to believe there have been serious cases of sexual harassment going on in this workplace and we'd like to hear if you've had any experience of it."

Rebecca sat and stared at the pair looking at her. Then slowly she began to register what they were saying. She blinked and licked her lips.

"Yes, I do know what you're talking about. The other day we had a new girl, a temp, to fill in for Justine, and I spoke to her after Mr. Porterman kicked her out of his office."

The two nodded encouragingly and waited.

"Well, when she came back to the pool, she was in tears and said she'd jumped out of her seat when he came around and put his hand on her while she was sorting his out-basket."

"Can you tell us, as close as possible to the exact words used, what she said, and can we record what you say?"

Rebecca looked a bit worried when they mentioned recording, but hesitantly she agreed and then became more enthusiastic as she started talking.

"Good, very good. And you say she jumped up from her chair when he touched her, on the shoulder."

"That's what she said. It was then I told her what he'd done to me."

"And that was?" encouraged Laurie

"Well, I won't go to his office at all anymore. You know, his hands are everywhere and he's such a sleaze, the way he looks at you. The time I filled in for Justine last year, he asked me to have lunch with him. I was quite flattered and we went to a lovely restaurant in town. And guess what? He sat next to me. Not opposite me but right where he could put his hand on my knee as soon as we got there. I was so embarrassed and I really didn't know what I should say, until finally I excused myself and said I had to go to the ladies. When I came back he had moved to the other side of the table, but then I had to look at him. You know, he's an ugly bastard, especially when he smiles. I actually think he's disgusting. Well anyway, that day we came back here and he's asked me out since then, but I'd never go. At the end of lunch that day he said we must keep our 'little outing' to ourselves, or others would know I was his favourite and then that would cause trouble and then I could lose my job. So now, I have nothing to do with him. So, has he been having a go at someone else, hey?"

"Yes, he has. Is there any more you can tell us from your own experience?"

"Well, I can't think of anything right now, but give me time and I might come up with more. What are you going do with this information?"

"For the moment we're going to collect and collate. After that, we'll see if we should go to a solicitor."

"Do you think there will be a compensation case, I mean, to go to the women he has harassed?"

"Possibly," Laurie said. "For now we'll be gathering everything we can, as quietly as we can, and as quickly as we can. It would help if you said nothing of this for the moment, because we don't want word to get out before we've had a chance to talk to more people."

"Oh sure, I understand. You can trust me. My lips are sealed," Rebecca laughed. "I'd better get to work before they notice I'm missing."

She jumped up and put her finger to her lips while trying not to smile as she left the room. Both Rose and Laurie could not help laughing after she disappeared.

The day warmed up, and by lunchtime, both Rose and Laurie were thirsty and looking for a chance to sit down. They returned to Laurie's office and sprawled on the chairs while drinking cola from the drinks machine.

"Bloody terrible stuff," said Laurie, after he had drained his can. "At least it gives you a hit and we need that now. Let's take a look at what we have so far." For the next half hour they went over the conversations they had recorded with three girls. "There's some pretty incriminating stuff there," Laurie said, as he looked at Rose.

She said, "I think this actually could be only the tip of the iceberg. We've had a fair turnover of staff among the young girls. Later today I think I will go to the accounts office and see if I can get some addresses of girls who have left in the past year."

"Good thinking, Rose. I'd like to talk to some of the men. They may know something and haven't bothered to speak up. Right!" Laurie stood with renewed resolve and turned to go out the door. His phone rang. "Yes?" As he listened, he frowned at Rose who was still sitting, finishing her drink. "Okay. I'll be there soon. Yeah, yeah, right away." He put the phone down.

"That was 'the king'– seems he has an urgent matter to discuss with both of us. Like right now."

"What shall we do?"

"Might as well get it over with. He can't exactly have us arrested for talking to people." Rose followed Laurie to the office of the Mayor.

******

At Keeala Resort, Di and Jim had taken a sandwich each and walked over to check on the progress on the other side of the lake.

"Such a beautiful day, and the way things grow around here it won't be long before all the development scars are gone. These trees look great," Di said, as she pointed to a row of native frangipani behind row of hibiscus, all new but looking so comfortable in their new environment. There was a mix of tropical exotics and natives, well designed to afford shade and enhance the privacy on the pathway to the new homes. "The lake's lovely and I'm dying to see how the water fountain is going to look," Di said enthusiastically.

Jim walked ahead, anxious to see the houses. Every house, offset from its neighbours for privacy, had a different design of both the structure and the landscaping. The gardens were unplanted but artist's impressions for each design ensured prospective owners could get a realistic impression of the finished effect. Builders were hard at work in the first house and they were working in the kitchen. Di's eyes widened when she noted the expensive finishes and fittings.

"This is going to be lovely," she said. "Are all the houses going to have these great finishes?"

"Of course," said one tradesman, looking at the couple at the doorway. "Take a look at the view from the back deck.

Then get a look at it from the master bedroom." They both walked through, taking care to step around the tools and debris littering the floor.

"Wow, I'm really impressed. Look at the lake and then all the way back to the mountains. Whoever gets this place is going to love it." Di had a broad grin, imagining waking up to the sun coming up over the lake. They continued their sightseeing and finally came to the end of the path.

"I was just thinking about the news we got today about Roger Sleighmen's death. He never got to see his great accomplishment," Di commented, as they walked back to the Clubhouse and their office.

"From what I've heard about him, he was more interested in the money he made, not creating a thing of beauty." Jim said, as he went to the notice board and began to tidy it; one of his 'obsessive compulsive' activities, according to Di.

"Well, that was fun. I wonder when the houses will be ready." Di wandered off to her own desk and started to sort through the waiting correspondence.

******

Colin Porterman's door was open when Rose and Laurie arrived at his office. There was an aura of heat coming from his room.

"Get in here," he shouted, as he confronted them. They both walked in silently and stood in front of his desk. "Well, don't just stand there! Tell me what's going on, and it better be good."

Porterman walked around the huge office, arms flailing, as though he was going to take off and fly.

Rose sniggered. She could not help herself and then put her hand to her mouth to prevent any more uninvited expressions escaping.

"You summoned us, I believe. Do you have a problem, Mr. Porterman?" Laurie was experiencing the quietest sense of joy at the sight of his long-term opponent in such a state of discomfort.

"You know exactly what I'm talking about, Lyall. I've had no less than half a dozen people in here today, all with stories about you."

"Or could it be stories about you?" Laurie tilted his head to the side, looking at the mayor as one might a naughty child.

"How dare you, you bastard. I know what you're trying to do. Well, it's not going to happen, you hear me?"

Rose and Laurie looked at one another across the room, trying to keep straight faces. He caught the looks and his face was livid. Porterman walked to the door and slammed it.

"Now, you listen to me. I'm not sure what your game is, but I've been in this place too long to be undermined by the likes of you. Both of you are only here as tokens. You're nothing but a couple of token greenies to satisfy the ultra-left-wing loonies. You have no power whatsoever! One word from me and you're finished."

Laurie put his hands up in the signal to stop. "Right, well now we know how you feel, you should know that this is only the beginning. We've had numerous, yes, numerous, reports of sexual harassment by you, from a group of the female staff. They came to us with their complaints and we have no choice but to pursue them. This matter is now in the hands of the police and the women involved have already had the benefit of legal counsel."

Porterman slumped on his chair and swivelled it with his back to them. He gave an almighty sigh.

Quietly, he said, "Get out."

They both left, squashing together to leave the doorway first. Outside they exchanged a glance as they made their way back to Laurie's office. There were dozens of faces turned in their direction and peeping out of office doors as they made their way down the corridors. As soon as they closed Laurie's office door they sat down.

"I think we'd better get over to the cop shop right away. Having told him we already have, I don't want to be caught short."

"I agree," Rose said, as she looked at Laurie. Her face was flushed and she looked as though she was about to explode. "Can you believe that? Never in my life have I ever enjoyed someone's discomfort as much as I have today. I had no idea I was such a vengeful person. So now, I know what it feels like. And I have to say, it's sweet."

Laurie nodded. "Rose, can you please ring Chris Young and ask him to meet me at the police station. I'm going now." He grinned at her and patted her on the back as he grabbed his car keys and strode from the office.

The phone rang, Rose picked up.

"Can I speak to Mr. Lyall, please?"

"Is that you, Isabel? It's Rose here."

Isabel went on to tell Rose about her own, very private, very embarrassing event with Mayor Porterman. When she had finished and Rose had written down all the relevant information, Rose told her that they were waiting on advice from the police,

"You'll be kept informed, Isabel."

"Thank you." She rang off.

The room fell silent and Rose turned to the window and looked at the landscaped entrance to the council chambers. A gardener worked away at pruning some big trees. *Cutting out the dead wood,* she thought. This led her to thoughts of flushing out corruption from the council, companies, and businesses. *If only it was that simple.* Rose began to wonder how many more complaints would surface now that word was out. *Would every girl who ever passed through the front doors be part of a class action compensation case? And who could prove otherwise, once the man's reputation was ruined? It would be their words, carrying the weight of evidence of their multiple complaints, against his discredited reputation. No one would believe the mayor, no matter how strenuous his denials. The court of public opinion was a powerful force with which to contend.*

Rose said it out loud, "Ex-mayor, Colin Porterman." *Yes, sounds great, but who would be replacing him? Maybe it's time for a female mayor in Westbridge.* She smiled and said, "Mayor Rose Magyari. Wouldn't Mum be proud?"

Chapter Twenty-Seven

Karl Simmens was an intuitive man. He could sense when danger lurked and he often removed himself from a potentially risky situation only moments before disaster fell.

His associate, Gene Gore, or 'the dickhead' or 'the hit man', as Simmens called him, depending on the circumstances, was the man he had often employed in the past to carry out the rough end of an agreement or contract. He was back in the country. He had been overseas, but had recently been seen interstate. Simmens knew he could very well turn up in Brisbane at any time. He knew this was not good news and had begun to make enquiries about contacting Gore. He hoped to warn him off. Gore had a connection to someone in high places, he was sure of that, and he was determined to find out who that person was.

Simmens spoke into his phone, "... For Gore to come back here now, he must have been satisfied that it was safe. I want to know the name of his contact. I want to go to sleep at night knowing this case is really closed." Simmens nodded at the phone, and then added, "No, I don't want to meet with anyone. I just want reliable information."

He rang off and sat pensively, hoping for some divine intervention that would give him a clue about his next move. Finally, he accepted that he would have to wait.

******

Pekalski was certainly going through a down phase, as he was beginning to think of it. Driving to work on a cool October morning, he wondered again if he should take some time off.

"Boss wants to see you, sir," said the receptionist to Pekalski, as he walked in the front entrance. He was startled and it took him a moment to realise she was talking to him.

"Which boss?" he asked.

"First floor, Inspector Bradley," she answered.

He diverted and turned to the stairs. Unlike the man that always took two stairs at a time, he quietly walked up the stairs and headed for the office at the end of the corridor. He did not visit this place often and it was not very familiar. He knocked.

"Enter."

"Detective Pekalski, sir."

"Come in, sit down. Haven't seen you for a while, Frank. How are you?"

"Well enough thank you, sir."

"Do I detect a little apathy or are you holding back your enthusiasm for the fun to follow?"

Pekalski stared back; it was then he realised just how down he really was. He had not a single response for the inspector. He would usually return quickly with a flippant remark or witty comment, but not today.

Bradley stood and walked around the desk. "I hear you've been doing some extracurricular work on the cold case of Jon Chamberlaine."

"Not anymore, sir. I was told to close it down. Not much point in beating my head against a brick wall." He fell silent again.

"I think I owe you an explanation, Frank; should have brought you into our confidence from the start, but we try to keep some information down to those who are on an absolutely need to know basis. I'm sure you understand."

"I do." Pekalski was beginning to develop the smallest tinge of interest in what the Inspector was saying.

Bradley walked back to his desk and picked up a file. He threw it into Pekalski's lap.

"It's all in there. The drug squad have been after a syndicate for several years; very professional and headed by Jack Noonan. They import and distribute large quantities of opium and have now branched out into fancy, recreational drugs. The drug boys were as close as they've ever been to nailing them, about a month ago. Then the operation dried up. Overnight. It all stopped. Well, that's happened before but this time we were just left hanging. We had an officer on the inside and he disappeared. We couldn't pursue him without giving ourselves away, so we backed off. You were not to know we were tracking a source within the Sleighmen Group, but that proved to have a dead end as well. It's possible Jon Chamberlaine stumbled on to some evidence before he was killed."

Pekalski looked up when he heard this last statement. His brain started to move into second gear.

"All roads did not lead to Rome, Frank. We think he was most likely in the wrong place at the wrong time. Anyway, we don't have the resources to keep up the vigil indefinitely, with no return on our effort. I think Noonan will keep for another day but we have a pretty sure link between the death of Chamberlaine and the new owner of the Sleighmen Group, Andrew Sleighmen."

Bradley went to his door and called for two coffees from his personal assistant.

"When Jon Chamberlaine headed the protest group, CARP, he was harassed by a certain cove from around here, Karl Simmens. He's a middleman and good at slipping out from under. Never gets his hands dirty but turns up in all the dirtiest places. We believe he employed another low-life to scare off CARP and perhaps Chamberlaine got in the way. Anyway, that particular low-life had left the country. We had no forensics on him and couldn't track him overseas." Bradley looked up as two mugs of coffee came in, gently held by a lovely young girl. Pekalski noticed her for the first time. She smiled at both the men and slipped back out the door.

"But now he's back." Bradley sat down with his coffee and a big smile on his face. "In the country, that is. We've been on his tail since he re-entered. I'm sorry we weren't able to share this with you at the time, but we were so close to Noonan that we could smell him. He also has several contacts in the Over-Fifties Resort. It's in our interest to leave them be; at least we have someone to monitor. As you are aware, they're more valuable to us as leads than behind bars for petty crimes."

Pekalski stood and walked around the room. His energy was stirring and he could not sit still.

"When you were chasing Chamberlaine's murderer, we were almost ready to close in on Noonan. But that's over now so if you're still interested you can pick up the trail of our newest immigrant." Bradley began to sip his coffee.

"Hmmm. I don't know what to say. Just when I'd washed my hands of the bugger, he turns up again. What have you got on this guy, any background?" Pekalski began to show an interest.

"Not much; has been an operator for some time, but no arrests. We've got one or two pictures of him, nothing good. I have a feeling he may be heading back here to Brisbane. He's been given assurances by an informant that we don't have a thing on him and the past is over. He suffers from a false sense of security right now, and I have a feeling he's coming our way. If you decide to pick up the case, I suggest you wait, let him come back to Brisbane and see where he takes you. His name is Geoffrey Gore – alias this, alias that – and so on."

Bradley took a breath and lounged back in his big, swivel chair. He looked long and hard at Pekalski and decided he was not mistaken. He would misplace his trust in this bloke. He had the strength of character needed to follow a trail to its conclusion. However, he did look tired.

"May I suggest you take a break? Keep in contact and come back on board in about two weeks. You can have this case exclusively and we'll help wherever necessary. It would be nice to put this murder case to bed. The syndicate has been around a long time and ain't goin' nowhere. Our greatest problem is tracking our man on the inside, and following the life and times of Andrew Sleighmen; that's our priority right now. What do you say?"

Pekalski smiled as he looked down at his empty hands. "I guess I owe someone an apology. I sort of nearly ripped his head off when he pulled me off the case."

"So I heard. He told me I'd lost him one of his best men."

"Did he say that? I was one of his best men? Even after I called him a complete shithead?"

"I guess you do have an apology to make. So you are on?"

"I'm on." Pekalski put his hand out and Bradley shook it heartily. They both smiled.

"I could do with a few days off though, boss."

"Certainly. Check in with my secretary and give her your details when you decide what you're doing. In the meantime, I'm sure your friend, 'Shithead', would like to talk to you."

Chapter Twenty-Eight

The Sleighmen Group business needed many changes. Since the sudden death of Roger Sleighmen, some of the employees felt a little uncertain about their position. While he had been a hard man to work for, at least most people knew where they stood. He was a ruthless and unforgiving employer and Andrew had, in recent years, been a buffer in some situations, but often had to act in a subversive way if he wanted to counter the hard effects of some of his father's decisions.

Now, Andrew was free to act according to his own conscience, though at times he was unsure of what that was. Being the leader of the organisation was a clear role and he slipped into it, roughly following the obvious guidelines set by his father.

"I feel like I'm damned if I do and damned if I don't," Andrew explained to Danielle. "I do want to run a tight ship but I don't want to become the merciless tyrant that was my father. When I look around at the different interests of the business I see lots of room for improvements, but none of them will make me any money, well, not directly, anyhow. They're things Dad would never do, but, in my opinion, are necessary."

"Are you talking about superannuation conditions and medical benefits for workers?"

"Partly, but I'm also thinking about flexible working hours and childcare provisions. Many other businesses have made allowances for these and a whole raft of better working and pay conditions that we're lacking. I don't want to overreact. I want to run a business I'm proud of. I'm not sure where to start though, love. I do know that some of the conditions I want to improve for our employees, while they will cost money in the short term, will bring much greater benefits to the company in the long run. I could never convince my father that a happy worker is a good worker."

"Well, may I give you the same advice as was given to me some years ago?"

"Be my guest." Andrew looked at Danielle across the dinner table.

"Nobody likes change. Well, most people don't, so do it gradually. A bit at a time and give those reluctant souls a chance to get used it all slowly. No matter what you do, there will be complaints and some people just love to whinge. Be consistent and don't try to take all the advice people will be so willing to give. You've got a good head, Andrew. Trust your judgment and you'll be fine."

"You make it all sound so easy." Andrew's expression softened and the worry lines, etched on his forehead, eased. "I'm so glad I have you, and David."

Andrew thought about the ongoing investigation into the death of Jon Chamberlaine. He wondered if he would ever be free of the guilt of his involvement. Sighing, he continued to pick at his food and he began to plan the changes he wanted to make in the business.

******

In the first week of October, Randell Thompsen died. For a time it looked as though he would pull through, but he never left the acute care ward and he died alone in the early hours of the morning.

Andrew contacted his ex-wife and two children but they were closed to any discussions about him. They had no idea about his double life and were mainly only concerned about the effects it would have on them, and whether they would be held responsible for his debts.

After reassuring them that it was not his motive, Andrew gave them his condolences and left feeling it may not have been the right thing to do. Going home, he made a decision to let go of anything he could not change and focus on the positives in his life. He let go all thoughts of Randell Thompsen.

******

"Andrew, a word please?" Muriel caught him going into his office the next day.

"Morning, Muriel, what's up?"

She smiled, a little smugly. "I'd like you to come and take a look at my latest figures." They walked together into her office and she pulled out her chair so that Andrew could sit in front of the screen.

He tried to decipher the many numbers and bottom lines in front of him. "So?"

"We have recovered all but two million dollars." She stood, looking over his shoulder and pointed to several sets of numbers that were of interest. "As well, I was hoping to discuss with you these short-term investments he's made. We can't access them now but when they mature we will, with a court order, be able to access that money also. I must say I'd be looking forward to see how much interest it has accrued. We may actually be able to recover some of our losses."

They looked at one another and both grinned from ear to ear.

"Sounds good to me, mate," said Andrew, as he stood and walked to the other side of the desk. "You should be very pleased with yourself. I certainly am – with you, that is." Andrew shook her hand and then stood thinking for a moment, before he said, "Muriel, I want to advertise several new positions."

Muriel looked up and stared at Andrew, her thoughts racing.

"What did you have in mind?" Muriel was concerned she would not like what she was about to hear. Since Roger's demise, she had been acting in the position of General Manager, previously held by Neale Simpkin.

Andrew said, "I had a call from Neale last night. He was fishing around for information. I have the impression he's not too happy with his new job and since Dad is out of the picture now, he probably wants to come back."

Muriel held her breath. She thought about how much she was enjoying her new, albeit temporary, position. She was in the office, most mornings, just after seven, and often still there twelve hours later. Her dedication was beginning to show, but some staff members had proved difficult and resistant to her effort. She continued to stare at Andrew, not wanting to pre-empt what he was going to tell her.

Andrew smiled, and asked, "What's wrong?"

Muriel shook her head and returned his smile, "Sorry, I think I was wandering off, in my own world."

"Well anyway, I was hoping you would give consideration to the permanent position."

"Me?"

"Yes, of course you, Muriel."

Again she stared, mutely, and then a slow smile spread across her pretty face.

"I'll be honest, Muriel. I'm looking for someone who's extremely smart, loyal, and hard working, innovative and personable. And that's you."

Muriel beamed. Never in her life had she felt so complimented. "Are you serious, Andrew? You're not having me on?"

"Not about anything as serious as this. It's in the interest of the business and everyone involved to have a great General Manager. That's what I see in you. I can't believe you've been here twelve years and have been so overlooked. We could have, all this time, been taking advantage of your many talents. Instead, you were working away in the background, and, may I add, for a pittance. Do you need time to consider my proposal?" Andrew bent down and wrote some numbers on a slip of paper. "That is what I would like to offer you to start and of course, there would be bonuses." He pushed the note across her desk with an enquiring expression.

She stared. Her mouth fell open.

"Of course, it is negotiable if you're not happy. We could make a few other considerations," Andrew said.

"No!" she snapped, as she looked straight into Andrew's puzzled face.

"Oh. Well, what would you consider fair?"

"I … I mean, I don't want to negotiate. That is much more than I could ever expect to be worth. You have to consider I am new to this job and have yet to prove myself. You can't give away all our profits to greedy management."

Andrew roared laughing. He sat back and almost choked on his own mirth. He rocked form side to side and eventually steadied himself, eyes streaming. He grabbed for a tissue on the big desk and wiped his eyes.

"If you're as tough in all your dealings, we're set to make a fortune. I can retire right now. Might as well go home and let you take over completely." Andrew sighed and settled, still smiling.

Muriel began to see what he was talking about and chuckled. "I was just testing you," she said. "I would hate to think I'm always so predictable."

"Well, you're definitely not that. You're obviously unaware of your own worth and that's something that you must change right away. Put a high value on yourself, and others will also. I've come to see what a valuable person you are, Muriel. You've kept things going here, with no preparation and no guidance. I've seen many improvements and I like the way you operate. There's so much we need to discuss, but first I want to know if I can have a contract written up. Naturally, I want you have input into it. We can call our legal eagle today, and get started on it. What do you say?"

"I say, yes!" They shook hands and stood, nodding and smiling in mutual agreement.

Chapter Twenty-Nine

Heads together and walking in unison down the front steps of the police station, Laurie Lyall and Chris Young discussed the statement they had just made. It had taken three hours for them to complete and it involved making a comprehensive list of witnesses for the police to interview.

Chris had been well prepared and had the assistance of a QC in his research and drawing up of all the relevant material. They knew they had to get it right the first time and Porterman's legal team would pounce on even the slightest mistake or loophole.

"I can't imagine what it's going to be like when I get back to work." Laurie had a slight smile on his face as they turned toward their respective cars, parked on the street. They shook hands. "What if I continue to get more complaints, Chris? I'm beginning to feel like we've opened Pandora's Box."

"Just take a statement and document it and then send them along to the police. This whole thing could end up bigger than Ben Hur. Politicians always attract a big crowd and lots of publicity, especially this one. I wonder who he'll take down with him."

"Indeed, the mind boggles. As long as we expose the bastard for what he is and remove him from his position, I'll be happy." They both hesitated before getting into their cars.

"Laurie, have you considered running for the position yourself?"

A grin spread across Laurie's face. "I have. As a matter of fact I've been approached by a business group and CARP with offers of support."

"We should keep that under wraps, for the time being," said Chris. "Can't look as if you have an ulterior motive."

"Absolutely. I can't afford to let my own ambition get in the way of prosecuting a very worthy cause."

"Well, I know you know what you are doing; the publicity won't do me any harm either, just quietly." Chris smiled as he put his foot down and took off back to his own office.

******

Colin Porterman was aware of the potential disaster on his doorstep. "I need to get an action plan together, right now. This thing could break by this afternoon and I'd better to be ready." He spoke to his publicity advisor, a man who had been with him many years and they had been a winning team.

"I don't think you realise, Colin; we can't just explain or bluff our way out of this. There'll be police charges to answer. I've no idea yet how many and the media will devour you. You need a very good lawyer and you need him now.

Perhaps you should consider one of the female persuasion. That would suggest how much respect you have for women, to begin with."

Porterman began to feel he could not breathe. He stood in his office with his hands on his hips, eyes wide, and his chest rising and falling as though he had just run a marathon. He stared at the man speaking to him. "This is bad, isn't it?"

The other man nodded.

Porterman began to think about an escape. He suddenly saw himself getting on a plane for Asia and getting lost in the backstreets of some city teeming with millions of people. He sat down, holding on to the arms of the chair, his breathing still ragged, his mind racing.

"What will you do?"

"Piss off," said Colin.

"Where to?"

"Wherever there's no extradition. Africa, maybe?"

"Look, mate, I'm not sure about how serious these charges could be. However, if I were a mayor and had heard there were so many sexual harassment charges about to be thrown at me, I'd start running. Why wait around for the axe to fall? Unless, of course, you believe you can fight this case. Do you think you stand a chance of defeating the charges? Are they true? No, don't tell me, tell yourself."

Porterman was shaking his head, almost as if he was coming out of the ocean and shedding the water. He stood up and paced around the room. "Fuck, fuck, fuck! Those bloody bitches. I've been set up; I can see it all, completely set up."

He started scratching his face, his head, and his arms. He started to cough, could not catch his breath. He began to wheeze and tremble.

The publicity consultant rushed over and helped him to sit. "Stop, relax, you're getting yourself into a state. Sit here." He reached for the decanter on the sideboard and poured the other man a half tumbler of whisky. Porterman gulped it down and coughed again. Finally, he began to take deep breaths and attempted to get a hold of himself.

Silence fell while the two men sat and contemplated the situation.

PR man said, "What have you got to stay around for, if you are convicted? Do you like this place so much that you would possibly go to jail and come out to face a life of ignominy. You have no wife or family to tie you here. You're free to go, and wherever you might end up, a little largesse will always buy friends of some description. Look, mate, the more I think about it, the more I feel you should pack up and move on. Even if you're cleared, you don't stand a chance of getting re-elected after a scandal like this. You've got plenty of money and I'm sure you've stashed some of it away for a rainy day. Speaking of which, Colin, you may want to think about how you came by a lot of it. There are many people out there who've been hurt by you and your back-room deals, and I'm sure they wouldn't think twice about kicking a man when he's down. Look, this sexual harassment stuff might be the least of your worries." The PR man sat and stared at his old associate.

Porterman stared into the distance for a moment, and then focused his vision on the phone at the corner of his desk. He picked up the handset with his left hand, and slid the magnifying index selector on his flip phone directory with his right. He selected 'T', pressed the bar, and the page popped open. He slid his index finger down the list of telephone numbers and stopped at 'Travel Agent'. He dialled the number and made a booking for late that afternoon to Port Moresby. Colin Porterman suspected he was the only one who knew about his indiscretions with a certain young girl employed in the office last year. He had paid her off, but she still lived on the Gold Coast. He wondered what prevented her from coming out now. With her, it had been a case of sex with a minor. He could also cast his mind back to what a girl had called rape; that disgusting word. She had accused him but he had managed to convince her he would counter accuse her of prostitution. Porterman knew there was a lot more beneath the surface that he could not afford to have brought into the open.

His mind raced with possibilities and he began to feel cold. He knew what he must do; he had a lot less choice than others might realise. He rang his driver and told him to bring the car round the back of the building.

"Be discreet," he told the driver.

He said to his PR man, "I'm going home to collect my passport and then I'm going to the bank. I'll make it worth your while if you cover for me. I'll need a head start, and if everyone thinks I'm in the office, they won't be looking for me."

"Sure," agreed the PR man. "I'll say you're in a meeting and take messages. Send your secretary on an errand. Only you and I will know you're on your way to the airport." They took a last knowing look at one another.

Colin Porterman saw his immediate future in front of him. He felt steely cold and yet galvanised into action. He would go to New Guinea. It could be a temporary refuge. Porterman judged that extradition would be unlikely, certainly in the short term. Anyway, he thought, in the time it would take to prosecute that procedure, he would have already moved on. A sense of excitement began to rise up inside him and his mind jumped from one scene to another. He had enough money now, and he knew certain people who would help him access more money after he left the country. He had a desire to travel, and now this was his opportunity.

"I'd like you to act as my agent, to sell the house after a while and liquidate other assets. I'll be in touch when I get settled and you won't be sorry for your effort, I promise." The men shook hands and Porterman slipped out quietly, pointing to the toilet when he passed his secretary. He heard a conversation with the secretary and his associate.

"Mr. Porterman has an article he would like you to pick up from the Post Office..."

The soon-to-be ex-Mayor disappeared out the back to his waiting car. His fleet-footed movement belied the size of the man.

Chapter Thirty

After a couple of weeks, Detective Frank Pekalski returned to duties. Something drew him back to the scene of the crime. He wandered around the new development and was suitably impressed with how well it was all going. He forgot about the bones of Jon Chamberlaine temporarily, and wandered from one new home to another. Like others, he enjoyed the walkways and gardens, the variety of design and size in the homes. He walked around, constantly surprised by the high standard of workmanship and finish. He talked to the workmen.

Finally he found himself back at the park that had previously been the bone burial ground. He once again brought to mind what might have happened to end the life of the protestor. *What was Chamberlaine doing here alone? Was he killed somewhere else and then dumped here? Was his death directly connected to his involvement with CARP?*

Pekalski had once again gone to look at Chamberlaine's Jeep and his personal belongings. He tried to understand what the man had done to upset someone enough to want to murder him. Or, had it been accidental? All these thoughts and more jostled for space in his head. His phone rang and he walked out into the sunshine to answer it.

He listened intently, and then said, "I'll be back at the station in ten minutes."

He moved off to find his car, and looked over his shoulder at the beautiful views he was leaving behind.

"There was a message left for you, sir." The young, female police officer handed Pekalski an envelope. "Brought in by a cab driver – said it was left on his passenger seat."

"Thanks." Pekalski took it and walked to his office. He had a sense of foreboding and did not rush to rip it open. He sat at his desk and finally opened the seal. A typed note on an A4 sheet read, *If you are interested in information about the death of Jon Chamberlaine, go to the 'Fossicker's Bar' of the Westbridge pub this afternoon, at two.*

"Well," Pekalski muttered, "what have we here?"

He made it his business to be at the bar ten minutes before the allotted time. He sat with his back to the wall where he had a good view of the door and most of the room. Five minutes after the deadline, he heard a voice.

"I hear old Roger Sleighmen died recently."

Pekalski swung around to see a nondescript, middle-aged man dressed in soiled work clothes sitting on the stool next to him. Shaggy, untidy curls of brown hair escaped from the confines of a baseball cap, worn back to front on the man's head.

"Did you know him? Are you the one who sent me the invitation?"

"Yes, and yes. The individual you're looking for left town, but now he's back. How much is it worth to you?"

"In my business, one good turn deserves another. No money, mind you, but you may have a little problem we can help you with. How does that sound?"

"I'd feel a lot better if I didn't have those traffic fines coming up."

"I have no reason to think that can't be arranged. What have you got?"

"Karl Simmens – middle man. Set up the deal with Andrew Sleighmen to scare off the protestors - back when they were building the first section of Keeala Resort. Simmens passed the job on to Gene Gore. He'd just returned from an overseas trip. Gore did the job."

"Where is he now?"

"Lives in the Valley somewhere; probably with his brother at Tenth Avenue. That's where he used to hang out."

"How did you know I was after him?"

"Simmens told me. He's worried Gore will take him down as well. He'd like to see Gore out of the picture. Simmens is into plenty of dirty deals but draws the line at murder – has a strong sense of self-preservation and an aversion to enclosed spaces."

"So the only reason you're telling me all this is to get rid of parking infringements?"

"My sister is involved with Gore and he's bad news. I want to see him off the street."

"I'll need your name if you want those tickets taken care of."

The man passed a slip of paper across to the detective. "I'd appreciate that," he said, as he winked.

While Pekalski looked down at the name, the man slipped out from behind the table and disappeared out the door. *Okay*, thought the detective, *looks like I go for a drive and see if I can find Mr Gene Gore.*

The sun shone and was an indicator of the long, hot summer on its way. Pekalski looked around for his informant friend but the street was almost empty. He began to plan.

Some computer crosschecking did indeed turn up a Morris Gore in The Valley. Pekalski drove to the address and staked out the house. A couple of hours later, two men turned up together in an old Holden Commodore. They seemed to be joking and laughing when they parked and looked up and down the street. They entered a rough looking, semi-detached weatherboard house in a line of similar buildings. They obviously had not noticed the detective parked discreetly around the corner. Pekalski drove off and made his way back to the station.

"An arrest warrant so soon? What grounds?"

Pekalski pulled the name of his informant out of his pocket. "I have a friend; I think I can convince him to tell us what he knows. Also, Simmens will be a little more co-operative once he knows we have connected him to Gore."

"Go for it," said Inspector Bradley. "I think you're right about Simmens being ready to cave in. He's all bluff and won't risk time in prison to protect Gore."

The next day, Pekalski was set to go. With a two car back up team they made their way to the Morris Gore's house and the three cars pulled quietly into position.

Pekalski signalled to the last car to block the lane that ran alongside the house. Next, he waited while three officers took up position behind the fence. Three more spread out in the front. He walked up and knocked on the door. There was no response. Pekalski counted to ten, and raised his hand to knock again, but the door opened slightly.

Gene Gore stood staring at Pekalski. He had no idea who he was looking at until the movement of one officer in his field of vision attracted his attention. He reacted instantaneously. He slammed the door shut, turned, and ran for the back door. He was through and out in the yard in seconds, making for the fence. With his hands ready to vault over the top, he saw the police moving on the other side.

"Stop! Police!"

He turned again, looking for another exit, but came face to face with Pekalski and two more officers. Just as he pulled his shoulder back to take a swing, one of the officers grabbed from behind and wrestled him to the ground. Handcuffs clicked, and Pekalski yanked him upright.

"Christ, if only they were all that easy," Pekalski said, with a grin to his mates.

Back at the station, Pekalski handed his charge over to be processed and locked up. "So, I'm sure you're feeling pretty pleased with yourself now," Inspector Bradley said, as he stood rocking on the balls of his feet, with his hands in his pockets.

"You could say that. I could not have done it without a little help from an anonymous tip off though. He stepped up at exactly the right moment."

"Your policing had a bit to do with it too, my friend. Why don't you share the good news with Shithead? I hear that's his new nickname now – really caught on."

Pekalski cringed, then smiled and said, "Think I will, sir" He turned and headed down the corridor to his superior's office.

Gene Gore's brother, Morris, came in that afternoon with a lawyer and they discussed the possibilities. Gene Gore cursed the fact that he had come back to the country, only to be picked up almost as soon as he hit the ground. He had believed he would be safe, but was sure someone had dobbed him in. He decided that if he did go down, he would not go alone. He had been paid to scare off a protestor, and through no fault of his own, had ended up killing the man.

"Murder! And that's a fact, Jack." Pekalski looked down at Gore, who had thus far been uncooperative with the questioning.

Gore opened his mouth and then shut it again. He was about to tell all, but reminded himself of what his counsel had just told him. He admitted to nothing and said 'no comment' to all questions.

Later that day, he was charged and remanded in custody. He was going to have lots of quiet time to decide what he wanted to say in court. Gore was aware that Simmens was going to be a witness for the prosecution, and he wondered if he could make a deal with the prosecution as well, in relation to Andrew Sleighmen.

Too late. They picked up Simmens the same day. They charged him with conspiracy to commit a crime in a situation ending in death. Simmens had immediately implicated Andrew Sleighmen as the person who employed him to intimidate Jon Chamberlaine.

******

As Danielle Hudson buckled David into his car restraint, she heard someone walk up behind her. She swung round to see two uniformed police officers and another man in a suit, standing, waiting for her to finish.

"Danielle Hudson?" the man in the suit queried. He flashed his ID.

"Yes, I'm Danielle Hudson. What's this about?"

The man in plain clothes introduced himself and the other two officers. "We are looking for Andrew Sleighmen. We believe this is his present address."

"That's right, but he's at work. Can I help you with something?"

"Thank you, no. We believe he may be able to assist us with our enquiries about a certain matter."

The detective interrupted Danielle as she began to give them Andrew's office address. He said they had it, and would proceed there shortly. They thanked her and left.

Danielle punched in Andrew's mobile number at work.

"Hello, my darling; to what do I owe such an early morning call from my beloved?"

"Bad news, Andrew. I just had the police here, and they're looking for you to ask some questions. I don't know what about."

A long silence ensued as Andrew's thoughts tumbled – then hesitantly, he said, "Okay, thanks. I'll call you later when I know what it's about."

He was afraid he already knew exactly what it was about. He hung up and immediately dialled the number of his solicitor. He drummed his fingers impatiently, as his call travelled through reception, personal assistant and finally to the man himself.

"This is James Donaldson. How may I help you?" Andrew was quick to explain his situation to the solicitor and felt confident he was talking to the right person. James had been involved in more than one criminal proceeding with the elder Sleighmen, and the outcomes had been positive. Donaldson told Andrew he would try to get to Andrew's office in time for the police interview.

When the police arrived, James was sitting opposite Andrew, taking notes. After the usual introductions, they began to question Andrew about his association with Karl Simmens.

Following his solicitor's direction, Andrew, as far as was possible, and without incriminating himself, attempted to answer all questions truthfully. Within moments of his answering the first few questions, it became clear to Andrew that was not possible. The fact that Roger was now dead meant that Andrew could share the responsibility of the crime with his father, but this did little to reduce his own complicity. He acknowledged he had sought out Simmens with the intention of 'scaring off' the protestors. He said he had no expectation of Simmens committing any violent acts.

They reached a point where all conversation stopped. James Donaldson agreed that a crime was committed, but emphatically denied his client's intentional involvement. He suggested Andrew had been drawn into a situation of which he was unaware, and for which he had no responsibility.

The investigating detective would not accept that argument. He arrested Andrew and later charged him with conspiracy to do bodily harm.

That night was one of the worst in Andrew's life. He had so much to lose if he went to jail – not to mention the fact that his son would grow up knowing his father was a criminal.

Chapter Thirty-One

Aaron Noonan had spent some of the last month in Vietnam, surfing. He stayed at Vungtau, and took advantage of the good weather and great waves. Having to stand down temporarily was no great hardship for him, and he continued to make contacts and work behind the scenes to keep the channels open. Now it was time for him to go back to work. With one phone call, he set the ball rolling again, and released the backlog of drugs on the unsuspecting public. 'Released by popular demand', he enjoyed saying, when he made contact with his Australian connection.

Aaron spoke to a young woman, passing herself off as a tourist. He had connected with her before, and she handed him several envelopes from Mikaila in Brisbane. He said, "We had to cease all our operations for the past month. The drug squad is always there, but we discovered an undercover cop. We had to lie low until he was disposed of and new links made."

"Yeah," she said, "I know. It has created lots of problems at home, but releasing this shipment now will come just in time. I hear Jack was beginning to think about retirement. Fine for him, but we have a whole lifetime to make a living. Does he know you and Mikaila are an item?"

"Not unless you tell him, sweetie, and I can be pretty resourceful if I'm doublecrossed. Do you know what I mean?" Aaron looked almost malevolent.

"Oh, for shit sake, back off. It was just an honest enquiry. I don't want to interfere in young love. If I'm carrying love letters, I just want to know what to do with them if I'm caught."

"Ditch them, naturally. They aren't love letters, anyway. What do you think mobile phones are for?"

"Yeah, yeah, forget it. Don't worry, I saw they were sealed and although it goes against all my principles, I haven't read them."

"Lucky for you," said Aaron.

The pair finished their business and parted. Drugs would continue to flow into Australia from Vietnam and Indonesia as long as Aaron Noonan and his family operated, and were protected by the contacts they had so carefully cultivated in politics and business.

Aaron opened the carefully sealed, coded letters from Mikaila who worked in his Uncle Jack's office. She too was sort-of related. Her late mother, Lauren, had been Jack's second wife. Jack had continued to treat Mikaila as a daughter after Lauren died. He had no idea his nephew Aaron and his stepdaughter were lovers, with big plans for their future together. Mikaila had access to all Jack's secret correspondence, and she transferred anything that would be likely to be of interest to Aaron, to him through the network of couriers. On his last visit to Australia, they had agreed on plans to branch out alone, when the time was right. That time would be when Aaron had enough money to set up somewhere else, beyond the reach of his family.

Jack had little love for anyone, but Mikaila and Aaron were special to him and he had no idea that his loyalty and trust were the important factors that they depended upon to betray him.

******

At Keeala Resort, the next shipment would be welcomed by Allen Sinclaire and further down the line by Kevin, the sometimes gardener. Kevin had already identified two new hideouts for his cache of drugs. He always got his supply directly from Allen and passed it to another pair of hands at regular intervals from the back gate. No names were ever mentioned, just whispered prices and dates. Allen and Kevin breathed a sigh of relief when the drugs arrived, hidden in the container of furniture. Once again, the regular flow was restored.

******

The work on the new development was coming along nicely, and both Jim and Di stood admiring the final touches going in. The days were getting longer, and the warm, sunny weather allowed the would-be buyers the pleasure of a good look around.

"If I were living here, I think I'd choose this one, here, closest to the lake." Di pointed and Jim nodded.

"Personally," said Jim, "I'd prefer the view to the mountains. It changes so much with the weather – sometimes grey, and then misty with the rain – and on days like today, it sparkles and the trees are so green." They both nodded and wandered on further, smiling to everyone passing by.

"I think I'm starting to get a handle on this place, at last," Jim commented. "It would be good to know that all the trouble with the death of that protestor was over. I wouldn't mind having a little more insight into our employer as well. It's strange how we have seen so little of him. Maybe now the old man is dead, perhaps things will change?"

"Hmm, maybe. I still feel there is a strange group of people living here. Not everyone, mind you, but some of them are quite weird."

Jim looked at Di sideways; he decided not to pursue his wife's idea of weird. He was having a good day, an uncomplicated one. He looked up when he heard his name called and saw a man striding toward him.

"Hello, Detective Pekalski. So nice to see you. Or is it?" Jim smiled.

Pekalski looked first at Diane. His eyes lingered a fraction of a second longer than they should have, as he appreciated her attractiveness. He then looked at Jim, who waited to gain his full attention. "Yes, it is a good day. We have finally made some headway with our investigation into the death of Jon Chamberlaine."

"That so? Well, do tell, who buried all those indigenous bones and murdered that man?"

"Ah, well, some of this is still speculation, but we have made some arrests, based on confessions. We now know that Mr. Andrew Sleighmen, your employer, made contact with a person and organised to have him link up with yet another contact to threaten the head protestor. If you get my meaning?"

"Go on," said Jim, wide-eyed.

"We had enough evidence to pick up Sleighmen, and he now languishes in a jail in Adelaide, awaiting extradition to Queensland. We also have the middleman, Karl Simmens, who is now awaiting Her Majesty's pleasure and convenience in jail in Brisbane. Finally, keeping Mr. Simmens company, we have Gene Gore, who says he accidentally shot Jon Chamberlaine in a scuffle over a gun. The gun was taken to the scene by Gore, to convince Chamberlaine of the seriousness of the situation."

"Dear God, this is all so scary," exclaimed Di. "What about the bones?"

"Yes, well they were found by the excavators when clearing the land for the first development. The particular operator involved knew not to inform the authorities. He did however contact Mr. Simmens, indirectly. Simmens was instrumental in organising the dumping of the indigenous bones. They had been unearthed from a burial site accidentally, and finally reburied near the lake. It was convenient. At that time, there were no plans to develop this land. When Gore accidentally caused the death of Chamberlaine, he thought the body would not be detected if it was unearthed with the other skeletons."

Jim summarised for Pekalski. "So, Gore had no intention of killing anyone. It was an accident – and he covered it up by burying the body with some old bones. Will he go down for murder?"

"Hard to say. If you carry a gun, you have to accept responsibility if it hurts someone. By the same token, if you threaten or pay someone to threaten someone else, you have to accept the responsibility for the outcome."

They stood together in the sunshine, all wondering how it would feel if it had been any one of them.

"So, I'm here to tell you that we have a hearing pending, several in fact and then perhaps some closure to this terrible event."

"You must be feeling pretty pleased with yourself, Detective Pekalski." Di looked at the policeman.

He smiled and agreed. "I'm very glad I was able to be part of the conclusion to this case. I actually feel for Andrew Sleighmen. He was caught between his greedy father's ambition and his need to please the old man. From what I know of Roger Sleighmen, he never approved of his son's actions and Andrew would have been unlikely to get his approval."

They all walked together along the path leading back to the Clubhouse and office. It was not in Pekalski's brief to make any comment about the drugs being moved around the resort, under the noses of the managers. That was a subject for another day, and Pekalski did not want to risk getting the managers involved at this particular time.

"What do you think will happen to the resort now that the owner is incarcerated?" asked Jim, as they stood near the car park.

"I haven't a clue. That is chapter two. I presume and we shall all wait and see the outcomes of the trials." Pekalski took himself off, happily.

"There is quite a change in that man," Di observed.

"Yes, indeed," answered Jim.

Chapter Thirty-Two

Colin Porterman did not talk to his driver on the way back to his home in North Brisbane. His head was full of plans and he tried to prioritise from the moment he sat in the car. He knew the important issues would be in relation to setting up his access to money after he left the country. It would cost him, but although he had some other financial interests outside Australia, he had not anticipated needing the bulk of his fortune at such short notice. He could see how he could do it with the help of several old friends and, as his publicity manager so recently pointed out, friends could be bought.

"Stay here; keep the car out of sight. I'll be about half an hour and then we'll be off again." He almost leaped from the car, up the driveway and in his front door.

The driver punched in a number on his mobile phone. "How interested would you be in the movements of the Mayor, Colin Porterman?"

"What sort of movements do you mean?" answered Laurie Lyall, from his office.

"I'm just now waiting outside his house. He will be back in a few minutes, and then we are off to places unknown. What's that worth to you?"

"A great deal." Laurie thought quickly. "When he comes back to the car, can you leave this line open on your mobile phone? If I could listen in and keep track of where you are going to, it could prove very valuable. I can't promise you anything for your service, but I do know you have your own scores to settle with the man, and this could be your opportunity. What do you say?"

"Okay. We'll talk later." He rang off, then sat back and thought about the unsettled business he had with the mayor.

Laurie rang Chris Young, "I've got a nasty feeling he is going to do a runner. We may have pushed him a bit too hard."

"Obviously he knows more about his sordid past than we do, and he can't risk having anything else come out. You should follow him. Keep me informed. By the way, I just had a call from a young lady who was working for Porterman a little over a year ago. She said she heard that several old friends had reported Porterman to the police and she said she had a sexual relationship with Porterman, and was coerced by him, when she was only a fifteen-year-old doing work experience at the council. She was reluctant to come forward because she has been paid off, but with Justine's support, she is prepared to make a statement. She will be going to the police station this afternoon."

"This is exactly what we want." Laurie's excitement could be heard through the line. "To get a witness to accuse him of a major crime would give us our immediate action. I wonder how reliable she will prove to be?"

"She impressed me. I'll give her a call right now and ask her to get herself down to the station immediately. Let's hope we will be in time, we don't want this bastard slipping through our fingers now."

"I agree, Chris, but if he decided to leave the country, that would be enough for me."

"That may be, but do you really want him inflicting himself on to other poor unsuspecting young girls – maybe in Asia, where life is cheap and girls can be bought and sold with impunity. No, Laurie, I would like to see this bastard stopped in his tracks. Right here, right now. We bred him; we should take responsibility for him. Let's not give up yet. I personally have no better fantasy than to see him languish in prison for a very long time, one where inmates take care of child molesters and sex offenders in their own way."

Laurie rang Justine and asked her to down tools and go with her friend to the police station. "For support, in case she has second thoughts and puts the visit off," he said.

"She's not really my friend, you know. I just knew her when she worked here. She was the youngest girl we had ever had in the secretary pool. She was a loner, and I remember that when she left suddenly last year, no one really missed her."

"That's fine, please give her all the support she needs now, and see it is done this afternoon. The sooner the better." Laurie was reluctant to tell Justine that he thought the mayor was going to disappear. Sometimes, telling Justine something was a bit like making a public announcement.

******

Colin Porterman's frustration rose as he rushed from one room to another, searching for his passport. He thought it was in his desk drawer, and then he remembered looking at it several months ago while he sat in bed. He had considered going on holiday with a lady friend, and they had joked about his passport photo and how it needed updating. *Where the fuck did I put the bastard?* he asked himself, as he pulled one drawer after another out and threw the contents on the floor. A flash suddenly reminded him to look in his brief case, the one he rarely used for work. *Ah, there you bloody well are.* He shoved it into his shirt pocket then went back to his bedroom to collect his laptop computer and several memory sticks. He stored them in his pocket, careful not to put them with his computer. He grabbed an overnight bag and began to pack. Undies and toiletries, a couple of shirts and some shorts. *Nothing too flash*, he told himself, *don't want to stand out in a crowd.*

He stood up and looked around the room. He walked from room to room, trying to imagine what he may consider essential tomorrow, when he woke up in New Guinea. He closed his eyes and, taking a deep breath, reminded himself that this was the beginning of the rest of his life. He turned and took the small photo of his mother and father from the wall. He rarely thought of them, but would like to think they were going on this journey with him. Something inside Colin Porterman told him his parents were the only people in the world who had ever loved him. He closed his bag and grabbed his keys as he made his way to the front door. He waved to his driver and the driver acknowledged, starting up the car and turning on his mobile phone. He rang Laurie

Lyall's number and heard him answer as he said, "All set Mr. Mayor?"

"To the airport please, and hurry, I have a plane to catch."

"International or domestic?"

"International."

The driver repeated the command loudly, "To the international airport it is, sir."

******

Justine and her friend walked away from the police station and decided to have a cup of coffee together. "We certainly deserve it after that ordeal," said Justine.

"Won't you be missed from work?"

"No, right now the boss is out, and what we are on about is the most important business of the day." She rang Laurie as promised.

Laurie had already rung the police station to tell them that Mayor Porterman was on his way to the airport and about to do a 'flit'. He was glad he had good relations with a few members of the force in Brisbane. Laurie rang Chris Young to update him and get his advice.

"It's in the hands of the Almighty now, Laurie. Don't worry, you've done your best, so let's see whether law enforcement can now do their bit."

Laurie and Rose sat brooding in Laurie's office, wondering if they had acted in time. They began to talk about urgent council affairs that they would need to address. With the Mayor gone, there would need to be big changes and that meant lots of work for everyone.

******

The driver lifted Porterman's bag and laptop from the boot of the car. "Would you like a hand, sir?"

"No thanks." He put a fifty-dollar note in the other man's hand.

"Sure." He pocketed the cash and watched his old boss hurry off to the departures line. He saw four uniformed police walked up behind Porterman and close in on him. He saw them speak and then Porterman pulled away, only to be grabbed by one officer and then handcuffs were placed on his wrists and he was diverted back the way he had come in. Their eyes met as the group walked past, leading the Mayor, and carrying his luggage. The driver looked away, unable to hold the terrified gaze of the captured man.

Chapter Thirty-Three

"You bastard, Joe!" Beryl looked down at the beach through her new telescope. Joe stood talking to two girls in bikinis. "Still at it, you old lecher," she spat.

She sat down and looked at the view from the big, sliding glass doors of their luxurious, new Gold Coast unit. They had bought the apartment with money gratefully laundered by the Sleighmen Group. The largesse was in recognition of the couple's assistance in helping the developers acquire the properties they needed for the expansion of Keeala Resort.

Shortly after they had moved in, Joe had discovered the delights of beachfront living on the Gold Coast. His wandering eye had given him new life and encouraged him to walk along the beach, morning and evening. His legs and his eyes followed the girls who seduced him with their youthful beauty in their short shorts and bikinis. Somewhere along the way, he had begun to think of himself as being attractive to them.

Beryl had bought herself a telescope and told Joe she was becoming a stargazer. The fool believed her. She regularly tracked her husband along the beach, watching him chat-up and possibly, from some of their reactions, accost young girls.

It was October. The weather was warm, so the intrepid walker was out and about early. On his return this Monday, just before midday, Beryl handed Joe a slip of paper, which he could not make head nor tail of.

"I am suing you for a divorce. I want the house and half the money."

"What money?"

"The little bundle you earned from the developers and managed to forget to tell me about."

Joe blinked. "How'd you know about that?"

"Well, my dear, you didn't marry me for my cooking."

"That's for sure," he admitted.

"So the next time I want to talk to a really stupid person, I'll just ring you."

"What?

"That was a quote from my friend, Marina, but you get the message. Okay?"

Beryl opened the bedroom door. All her soon-to-be ex-husband's bags were packed and waiting. "Here's the number of my solicitor," she said.

She walked to the front door and held it open. "I'm sure you can find yourself someone nice to bunk down with until this is all settled."

"Are you serious?"

Beryl smiled. "What do you think, lover boy?"

******

Laurie and Marian Lyall had worked hard in the weeks leading up to his election as Mayor. It was some weeks later when he took office and he celebrated his success with his many friends and supporters.

There were some disgruntled councillors, but they were mostly grateful that they still had a job. Only they knew the extent of the corruption they had been part of. Laurie knew he had plenty of time to sort out the dead wood and create the sort of council they could all be proud of.

"You did it!" Marian had said the night the count was finalised. "I'm so proud of you, my darling."

"Me too. I'm not naive enough to think we'll eradicate all the corruption and criminal activity, but any improvement is good."

******

Jim and Di did not get to meet their employer, Andrew Sleighmen, at the grand opening of the last stage of Keeala Resort. Muriel Jacobs was present to represent the owner. It was her first trip to Queensland. She planned a grand tour of all the Sleighmen interests since her boss was unavailable, and she had no idea how long this situation would prevail. Following his conviction as an accessory to manslaughter, Andrew Sleighmen was in jail and awaiting the appeal of his case. He felt hopeful that the time he had already spent behind bars would suffice when the appeals judge made his decision. For the time being, he would be going nowhere.

The main positive thought that helped Andrew cope with his ordeal, was of his family and his business. He believed he would survive and go on to take back the reigns of the company, which he had done so much to build up. He had the support of Danielle, who had become his wife while he was still free on bail.

"I'm told this will be the last resort built for the Sleighmen Group. I hope it will be the most successful for the owner and the most liveable for the residents and that everyone will be happy living here." A prolonged applause followed and the new Mayor, Laurie Lyall declared the luxury development, 'Open'.

The managers, Jim and Di Watersen, applauded along with the rest of the crowd.

"Thank goodness we've seen the end of all the troubles, Di. Now we can relax and get on with the job, stress free."

Di glanced at Jim. *I wish I had your confidence, my love.*

The End

Author Kumari and husband John live in an Over 50's resort in Queensland.

In their past careers, John was a business manager and Kumari, a registered nurse.

After their marriage in 1992, they combined their skills to manage retirement resorts in N.S.W. and Queensland. They used to joke that the many interesting characters and unusual situations they encountered would one day provide a wealth of material for a book.

When Kumari became wheelchair bound following foot surgery in 2010, she realised the period of physical inactivity presented her with a golden opportunity. She decided to weave her memories of those management years into a fictionalised story. The result was not one novel, but a series.

The series follow the trials and tribulations of the residents, employees and diverse characters of Keeala Resort. Kumari also introduces social comment about ageing issues and some of her characters draw her readers into a dialogue about the social and practical questions encountered in people's mature years.

Sixteen grandchildren fill in the spaces when she is not writing.

www.ingramcontent.com/pod-product-compliance
Lightning Source LLC
Chambersburg PA
CBHW070220030726
47505CB00006B/1744